Matt Wilson

STORY

FANTAIL PUBLISHING

AN IMPRINT OF PUFFIN ENTERPRISES

Published by the Penguin Group
27 Wrights Lane, London W8 5TZ

First published by Fantail Publishing, 1989

Copyright © Licensing Management International, 1989
All rights reserved

014 090154 X

10 9 8 7 6 5 4 3 2

Made and printed in Great Britain by
Richard Clay Ltd, Bungay, Suffolk

THE

Matt Wilson

STORY

Anthony Ellis

FANTAIL

chapter one

'Why have I got a Dad who's a bin man?'

Eleven-year-old Matt Wilson sat on the crest of a large sand dune and stared out to sea. A scowl sat uncomfortably on his normally fresh and open face, as he relived the morning's humiliations.

'Hey mate, what's the pong?' Matt could hear Lance Smart's idiotic chuckle as if he were back outside the General Store where it had all happened.

'Don't know, mate. But it sure is strong,' Lance's partner-in-crime Martin Dibble added gormlessly.

The two boys had blocked Matt's way as he'd tried to enter the weather-beaten old building. Both were slurping milk shakes.

'You'd reckon a bloke'd wash a bit more when he lives 'round rubbish all the time,' Lance followed up.

'Too right,' continued Martin. 'Not surprised

he smells. I mean, if your old man collects garbage all day, I reckon he passes the pong on to you.'

Matt bit his tongue. These two, at thirteen, were bigger than him; bigger by far. He wasn't going to risk a punch in the head. But Lance and Martin were on a roll. They were after a response, either tears or an outburst, and they weren't going to let up until they got one.

'Eh Wilson, what are you after?'

'I want to buy some milk.'

Matt mumbled the reply to Lance's needling question, not trusting himself to answer forcefully. If he didn't keep a firm lid on his feelings, he knew he'd say something that would get him into trouble.

'What?' Lance and Martin chuckled, exchanging delighted grins. 'What? We didn't hear you.'

'Mum wants some milk.' Matt could feel his anger rising.

'How come? What does she need milk for?'

The way Martin's grin spread across his face rang a warning bell for Matt.

'I've given them something they can use,' he thought.

'Why would he have to buy milk, Lance? You'd reckon his old man'd drain the bottles down the tip and bring the stuff home.'

'Yeah, mate.' Lance seized the opportunity. 'Must make life real cheap, havin' an old man like his. Look at his clothes, eh.'

Lance flicked the collar of Matt's worn windcheater with his forefinger.

'You can tell just by lookin' at 'em where his old man got 'em.'

'No knowin' what he gets down the dump,' Martin added. 'You even read about babies bein' found there sometimes. That where he got you from Mattie-Poohs? Did your old man collect you like all the other rubbish?'

That was it; the proverbial straw. Matt could hardly remember the next few seconds. All he knew was that one minute Lance and Martin were wearing stupid grins, the next they were wearing their milkshakes. A quick upswing, a hand on the bottom of each paper cup, and the sticky mixture of milk, flavouring and ice cream splashed into the bullies' faces. His instinct for survival instantly came into play. He took to his heels, the outraged pair in hot pursuit. Dire threats rang in his ears.

'We'll get you, dork.'

'You're dead, Wilson.'

So here he sat, his lungs still burning from the after-effects of flight and his face from the anger aroused by the recollection of their taunting. A seagull flew by, emitting a lonely cry into the sharp wind that blew across the Bay. He followed its progress and, as he did so, his eyes swept the view.

Summer Bay. This was home. He had grown up with the ocean that changed from a sparkling blue on sunny days to a deep and angry green when clouds gathered; with the sand that grated between his toes as he dug his feet deep to find the coolness beneath the surface; with the rocky headland of Stewart's Point, where the sea surged angrily; and with the wildlife sanctuary of the Wetlands, spreading away at the other end of the beach.

'You're a hero. You know that?' The voice that cut across his reverie belonged to a short, almost dwarfish powerhouse of delinquent energy called Bobby Simpson. She stood grinning at him for a moment, then dropped down next to him.

'Didn't think you had it in you, Mattie-Poohs.'

'Don't call me that,' Matt snapped before he could control himself.

'Sorry.' Bobby was instantly and genuinely apologetic. She liked the guy, despite the fact that they had little to do with each other. They were in the same class at Primary School but Matt hung around with a different crowd. He'd always been decent to her however and, in a school where she was treated like the local leper, that meant something.

'The name's Matt.'

'I said I'm sorry, didn't I? I saw what you did. Good on you.'

'They had it coming,' Matt replied. He didn't want her congratulations. What was there to congratulate him for? For putting his neck on the chopping block? For making sure that he'd be waylaid eventually and have the stuffing knocked out of him?

'If you want any help . . .?'

'What sort of help?'

'You know. An extra pair of fists or somethin'.'

Bobby's offer was well meant, but it rankled with Matt. 'What is it with me?' he asked. 'How come everyone sees me as a wimp?'

'Who says they do?'

'Of course they do. You can't tell me you don't. You think I'm so weak that I need a girl to do my fighting for me. Yeah well, I'm sick of it.'

Bobby picked up a shell and started to pull it apart. The little rebel didn't like heart to heart conversations. She had too many problems of her own to get more than casually involved in anyone else's. She'd only come down to offer him help in a punch-up, and here she was, faced with an outpouring of frustrated emotion. Well she didn't need it.

'Yeah, well maybe I do think you're a wimp. Maybe everyone thinks it. But they'll think it less after today. Unless you crawl back into your shell again.'

Her response was like a bucket of cold water that brought Matt sharply to his senses.

'Don't hide down here worryin' about when those two creeps'll get you,' Bobby continued. 'Go out and find 'em and have another go. They're about as scary as a Benjie movie. I'll be there to back you up. Show 'em you're not afraid and they'll never rag you again. No one will.'

Bobby was used to action. She took Matt's silent consideration as a rejection. And it infuriated her.

6

'Oh, I know what you're thinkin'. What good's her advice? How does she know what it's like bein' me? Why do you reckon I came down here, eh? Cos I *do* know. You reckon you're the only one with an old man you're ashamed of? I'm a lot worse off than you are. At least your old man's good and kind and works hard and comes home at nights sober. All he ever did wrong was take a job that dumb kids can make jokes about. Mine . . .'

She brought a world of distaste and despair to the word.

'. . . mine's on the dole, he beats up Mum and me, he's pissed half the time. How do you reckon I feel? The only difference between you and me is, my old man deserves the things they say about him and yours doesn't. You should be proud of him, even if he does stink when he comes home.'

The truth behind her words made Matt start with a sudden sense of guilt.

'I know what it's like to be ragged, all right.' Bobby concluded her call to battle. 'So let's go and knock some heads together and stop two of the biggest raggers dead in their tracks.'

Matt didn't quite know how he got there but, carried away on a wave of adrenalin, he found himself striding down the main street with Bobby at his side. She was right! Why not silence everyone by delivering another blow, swift and sharp, to the 'dynamic duo'? Fatman and Slobbin had it coming. And he and Bobby were going to do it.

They made an unlikely pair; the tall Nordic-looking boy and the squat young toughie, striding purposefully towards their destination – the disused bus-shelter that Lance and Martin had appropriated as their headquarters. An unlikely enough pair to cause Celia Stewart to swerve on her bike as she saw them coming.

'That lovely young Matthew Wilson with the likes of Bobby Simpson,' Celia thought. Here was a combination it was her Christian duty to split asunder.

'Matthew!' she called sharply. 'May we chat for a moment?'

'Rack off,' Bobby muttered under her breath.

'I've got something urgent to do, Miss Stewart.' Matt didn't want one of Celia's jabbering lectures to douse his enthusiasm for battle.

'It will only take a moment.'

'Ignore her,' Bobby hissed.

'You know how she never lets up. She'll just tag along if I do.'

Matt moved to where Celia waited, propping her bike against a tree. This didn't bode well for the brevity of her 'chat'.

'I know it's none of my business, but . . .'

How many times had Celia begun a conversation like this, proceeding to launch into her compulsive interference in the lives of others.

'. . . I dandled you on my knee, Matthew; listened to your baby mewlings. I feel this gives me the right to speak out.'

One of the problems with Celia was that you needed an interpreter to understand her.

'Suffer the children to come unto me.' She was always at her most dangerous when she quoted from the Bible. You knew she was really moving in for the kill. 'But even the tolerance of our Lord would have been taxed by young Bobby Simpson. Do you understand?'

'I might if you just said what you meant,' thought Matt, anxious to be away. But all he said was:

'I'm afraid I don't, Miss Stewart.'

Better to be a hypocrite and play the good little boy, than be stuck here for an hour getting a lecture on bad manners.

'Then I shall elucidate. It pains me to see

you walking the streets in the company of
Bobby Simpson. Especially as I have just
heard another shocking piece of news; that
you were involved in some form of fracas
with Lance Smart and Martin Dibble. You
have always been such a good boy, Matthew,
such a tribute to your dear mother and
father. And now suddenly to find you mixing
with the . . . how shall I put it? . . . less desir-
able elements in our little community . . .'

Matt switched off. He watched her mouth
opening and closing, pumping out enough
hot air to float a balloon. He glanced past
her shoulder to where Bobby was waiting,
pulling rude faces and doing an impressive
imitation of Celia in full flight. The act was
so comical, Matt had to smile.

'I wasn't aware I'd said anything amusing.'
Celia's face darkened with disapproval. She
turned and looked behind her, sensing what
was happening. Bobby was too slow in adopt-
ing an innocent pose. Celia flared.

'You, Bobby Simpson, run along. And thank
your lucky stars I don't give you what for.
Go, you wretched girl, before I really lose my
temper. Matthew will not be coming to play
with you, today or any other day.'

Her dismissive tone was like a red rag to a
bull. Bobby fired back.

'What business is it of yours, creature features?'

Celia flicked her head and snorted. She wouldn't deign to reply to this rude outburst.

'Come on, Matt. Let's go,' Bobby called.

Matt was torn. He was still as eager as before, but he'd been brought up to respect adults. It wasn't as easy for him to thumb his nose at Celia as it was for the habitually rebellious Bobby.

'What are you? You wimp. Oh, rack off then. I don't know why I bothered.'

Bobby started to move away, infuriated. She'd made an effort to help the guy, and here he was siding with a stupid old maid. All he had to do was say 'I'm going now'. It wasn't as if she was asking him to tell Celia to get stuffed.

'Don't blame me when word gets round you're a pansy.'

That did it. Matt could see the months of torment. All the laughing behind his back, the taunting to his face. 'Too frightened to stand up for yourself.' 'What are you, you big poofta?' And all the chorusing of his hated nickname, the one coined by Lance and Martin: 'Mattie-Poohs, Mattie-Poohs'. It rang over and over in his head. He made up his mind.

'Come back, Matthew. Come back this instant.' But Matt strode away, not even calling an apology for leaving Celia in mid-babble.

'You little beauty!!!!' Bobby whooped and punched the sky. The wimp had turned.

Celia's face resembled a beetroot, as her blood-pressure soared. Another decent young member of the community poisoned by that minion of the devil, Bobby Simpson. She leapt on to her bike and pedalled away, bent on a holy mission. What sort of Christian was she if she sat back and let a lamb from the Lord's flock stray into the brambles of delinquency? This and similar thoughts bounced about in her head, like the artificial flowers bouncing on her hat, as her bike bounced along the pot-holed road leading to Matt's house. She was not an interfering woman, she assured herself, but the boy's parents just *had* to be told.

Martin drew deeply on his cigarette and puffed amateurish smoke rings into the air above him. The shapes formed were recognizable enough as circles to impress the simple-minded Lance.

'How do you do it, Marty? Eh? Show us how.'

'No way, mate.'

'Oh jeez Marty, are you me mate or aren't you?' Life was a constant source of injustice to Lance.

'It took me yonks to learn it 'n' I went through bulk ciggies. You reckon I'm just gonna give the secret away?'

'Not even to a mate?' Lance whined pathetically. Martin nonchalantly blew another smoke ring as he turned to take in his friend's pleading gaze.

'We'll go over to the Yabbie Creek milk bar. I'll use it to pull mega-chicks. You can have the ones I don't want.'

'Yeah!? Oh wow!! Thanks Marty, you're a beauty.'

Lance sank into the corner of the shelter and savoured the anticipation, while Martin lay back on the bench and indulged in a lurid day-dream. He saw himself in Tony Poletti's Milk Bar, the focus of the Yabbie Creek teen set, filling the air with perfectly formed O's of smoke. Each exhibition of his skill drew a collective sigh from a group of scantily-clad girls, as if they were reading the letter which he had just floated.

'Oh, Martin, you're such a hunk,' breathed the cutest of the girls, as she draped herself around him.

Drip!

A drop of sticky wetness intruded upon this fantasy.

Drip! Drip!

He put his hand up to wipe his forehead.

'Hey Marty, the roof's leakin'.'

'I know dork-brain.'

Then the smell hit them. Martin looked at his hand. It was covered in a slimey, greeny-brown liquid.

'Oh yuck Marty, this stuff pongs.'

Martin looked up at the ceiling and saw another drop of the noxious substance forming above him. And then came the sound. A sort of . . . what? . . . scuffling movement on the roof. Something was up there.

'Must be cats mate, doin' their stuff up there. Let's get out of here.'

Martin got up quickly and led the way out, Lance close behind.

'If I get m' hands on the little mongrels I'll wring their necks. Dirty stinkin' cats.'

Meeow!

The sound came from above them, as they emerged from the shelter.

Meeow! Meeow!

Two sounds in harmony. One high, one low.

'That doesn't sound like cats.' Martin had only enough time to think the thought, before two streams of filthy, nauseating brew washed down over them.

'Oh puke.' 'Gross out.' 'Oh Marty, no.' 'Vomit making. Ahhh.'

They leapt around, trying to wipe the filth from their hair and eyes. Then they heard it. The laughter! There, on the edge of the bus-shelter roof, sat Bobby and Matt, laughing fit to burst.

'You don't have to have an old man who's a garbo to stink,' Matt crowed.

'Serves you right,' chorused Bobby. 'And that's just the start you dorks, if you don't lay off.'

'Brains rule, okay.' Matt felt euphoric. 'You can punch my head in if you like, but I'll always get you back ten times worse. It'll take days to lose the smell of that lot; the next lot, it'll take weeks. And the one after that . . . you'll never get rid of it. You want to stink for the rest of your lives, you just keep it up.'

'We'll get you, Wilson,' Martin roared.

'I don't reckon you will,' Bobby laughed. 'Not once you've thought it over.'

Matt and Bobby jumped from the roof and darted away. Matt couldn't resist calling back.

'If you want to know what it is, ask Nico Pappas' cow. Plenty more where that came from.'

He felt ten feet tall as he bounded off behind Bobby. For the first time in his life he had taken a stand against the kids who made his life hell, and the feeling was wonderful. And the best thing was, he'd done it on his own terms. Bobby had been all for going in with fists flying, but Matt knew that violence would get them nowhere. You just had to read the newspapers to figure out that violence didn't get anyone anywhere. A little thinking on his part had yielded a punishment that fitted the crime. Lance and Martin constantly heckled him for smelling like garbage. Let them see what it felt like to have people turning up their noses . . . literally.

'You're okay, Mattie-Poohs.'

Even Bobby's use of his once-hated nickname didn't worry him now. The afternoon's activities were a bond between them and if she wanted to call him that, so what? She was his mate now.

'You're okay too, Bob. Thanks.'

'For what? It was your idea.'

'You got me going though.'

'Yeah, well don't wimp out again. You'll have a reputation now. You've gotta live up to it, or you'll be back where you started. Check you later, killer.'

Bobby chortled as she strode off.

Matt hurried towards home, but his pace slowed as he approached his street. Bobby's words, initially so exhilarating, were starting to sour upon reflection.

'You'll have a reputation now. You've gotta live up to it . . .'

But what sort of reputation? As a lout on the level of Lance and Martin. Even Bobby, although he appreciated her help, was hardly someone he wished to emulate. He wanted the respect of the other kids, he wanted to be accepted; but on his own terms; just as he had wanted revenge on his own terms. The change in his fortunes was not as cut and dried as he'd at first thought.

When he turned into his street and saw Celia's bike leaning against the fence, his heart sank. He wasn't in the mood to face his mother's disappointment and Celia's inevitable outrage. His new status had to be thought through and a solution had to be found. He turned on his heel and headed for the beach.

'Here I am, back where I started,' he thought ironically. 'But with one set of hassles replaced by another.'

His eyes swept the bay, as he struggled to untie the Gordian Knot of his problem. He remembered his teacher telling them the legend of this knot. An ancient king had tied it. It was extremely intricate. The story went that the man who untied it would become king. Many had tried and all had failed. And then came Alexander the Great. He solved the problem with a single stroke of his sword. He slashed through the knot, thereby untying it in a way that no one had thought of before. And he became king.

Lateral thinking, his teacher had called it; not just following one train of thought, but jumping the track.

'That's what I've got to do,' Matt told himself. 'Think laterally.'

Far out, beyond the crests of the breakers, a young man straddled his surfboard, waiting for another set to roll through. Matt watched as the surfer sighted his next wave. He lay flat on his board ready to paddle, then swung himself into the swell, pumped his arms to make the momentum of the board one with that of the wave and stood upright to ride the foam-flecked monster. And then he was away with all the freedom of a bird, speeding across and down the wall of water, weaving forward, flicking back up, using the power of the ocean to fuel his flight.

Wow!!

'If only I could be out there with him,' thought Matt. 'If only I could do that. They'd have to respect me then. And for all the right reasons; for my skill and for my talent, not because I dumped muck on the heads of a couple of creeps.'

Slash! Suddenly the knot of his problem was severed. He could see the answer so clearly. And when his father asked him, the following week, what he wanted for Christmas, his reply was immediate and enthusiastic.

A surfboard!

chapter two

Poor Little Rich Girl. Amanda Taylor had heard the phrase so often in books and on TV, but she simply couldn't relate to it. It was almost as if the writers of novels and movies wanted to believe that wealth and happiness didn't go together. But they did. And she was living proof of the fact.

She looked in the mirror in front of her. At fourteen she had a flawless complexion; her shoulder-length hair was lustrous, blonde highlighted with faint flecks of red; her lips made a red and moist cupid's bow. Hers was a precocious beauty. She looked sixteen or seventeen. She'd seen girls like herself in American movies; the Prom Queen look they called it.

She ran the brush through her hair four more times – ninety-seven, ninety-eight, ninety-nine, a hundred.

'A hundred times a day; morning and night,' Mummy had always insisted.

Suddenly a cloud passed across her face. She tossed the brush away amongst the paraphernalia of her dressing table, rose, walked to the bed and threw herself down.

The pain of her mother's death was still very much with her, could still make sudden assaults upon her from the subconscious. Maybe she was a poor little rich girl after all. But no. Death affects all families, rich and poor alike. Whether you live in elegant Vaucluse or seedy Redfern, the death of a mother cuts just as deep. Despite the loss of this woman she had loved so much, she could still count her blessings.

She closed her eyes and breathed deeply. Rose Arbour, her mother's favourite perfume. She could conjure up the comforting odour even now, a year after the funeral; and with it, happy memories.

Mummy, Daddy and herself on the learners' slope in Zermatt. Her first skiing lesson. The three of them in New York. Central Park. Daddy showering them with the multicoloured leaves of autumn. Her and Mummy, at the top of the Eiffel Tower. Just the two of them. Her twelfth birthday. Daddy had joined them later at Maxims. Her first sip of champagne and her first taste of caviar. Caviar. The smell of fish. Fish. Fishing. A fishing-line. A fish dangling at the end of a line.

'Mummy, mummy, quick. Take it off, take it off.'

A memory from far back in her childhood intruded abruptly. She had no idea where it came from; it was just suddenly there. She was three. Mummy, Daddy and herself in a dinghy. They were dressed in scruffy, old clothes. They were fishing and she had made her first catch. She could see the blue of the water around them, see her mother's smiling face and could sense something. What? A happiness radiating from her mother that was greater than any she could remember.

'Daddy? Can I ask something?'

Bernard Taylor looked up from his copy of The *Financial Times*. His daughter stood in the open doorway of his book-lined, mahogany-walled study.

'Come in, darling.' He patted his knee. 'Of course you can.'

Amanda moved across quickly and slipped on to his lap, winding her arms around his neck.

'I just remembered something,' she said. 'I

was three. There was you, me and Mummy. We were in a boat, fishing. Where were we?'

She felt her father tense.

'What made you think of that?'

'I don't know. I was thinking about Mummy and then ... you know how you think of things for no reason? I was there, in the boat. Tell me about it.'

Silence.

'Please, I want to know. Mummy seemed so happy. I don't remember her ever being so happy. Why was she so happy then?'

Nothing could have prepared her for his reaction. She had never seen her father like this. He pulled her arms from around his neck, stood up, and let her slide from his lap.

'You've never been fishing in your life. You're imagining things.'

'But it seemed so real.'

'So do a lot of dreams. That's all it was, a day-dream.'

And then he softened. But Amanda could sense that he was forcing the change. She knew that he was lying. She also knew that now was not the time to pursue the matter.

'It's late darling. Off to bed. And no more silly dreams. Fishing!' He laughed derisively. 'The most boring pastime in the world. Your mother couldn't even stand the thought of it.'

He kissed her forehead and guided her from the room.

'Sleep tight.'

But she didn't. She tossed and turned, worrying at the image from her past. She could see the boat, her parents and the flat, blue ocean stretching to the horizon in front of her. If she could just turn her head to the right or the left she could take in more of her surroundings, perhaps recognize the place. But the more she tried, the less she could see.

Then, as she slipped into deep sleep at around four in the morning, another image surfaced from her subconcious. She could see a sign at the side of a road. A young woman lay on an air mattress, laughing as the waves danced around her. And emblazoned on the sign in huge black capital letters, the logo:

WELCOME TO SUMMER BAY

Amanda lived in a mansion in the fashionable Sydney suburb of Vaucluse. She attended school at SCEGGS, Sydney Church of England Girls' Grammar School, a training ground for the daughters of the wealthy. As she was driven along New South Head Road the next morning, making the journey from home to school, the blue waters of Sydney Harbour sparkled on her right hand side. Summer Bay. Would the water sparkle as brightly there?

That day, in her free period, she went to the library and found a map of the State. She knew instinctively that, as far as this matter went, she would have to search out her own answers. Her father had been his usual caring, jovial self at breakfast, but there was something; an undercurrent. She knew that any mention of Summer Bay would be unwise. He was not normally a man to have secrets. She couldn't understand. Why was he so closed on this one subject?

Summer Bay. Her finger touched the spot. There it was, tucked away on the Central Coast, an hour or so's drive north of Sydney. The name was in very small letters, squeezed between other towns whose larger and darker lettering attested to their greater importance in the scheme of things. Its closest neighbour to the north was Yabbie Creek and to the south, Yandawarra. What silly names Australian towns often had. There was a straight-forwardness to the name Summer Bay that endeared it to her immediately.

At lunchtime she slipped out of school, avoiding the gimlet gaze of the teacher on yard duty, and hurried across to the nearby public phones. She dialled the New South Wales Tourist Authority.

'Could you send me whatever you have on Summer Bay?' she asked. 'It's a small seaside town just north of . . .'

'I know where it is,' said the pleasant-voiced woman on the other end of the line, 'Though we don't get many enquiries about it, I must say. Looking to rough it these holidays, are you?'

'Yes,' Amanda lied.

She suspected that this was only the first of many lies she would have to tell before she had the answers she was after.

'Where should I send the material?' the voice from the receiver continued.

More subterfuge. She gave her address as care of the school. She couldn't risk her father seeing the Department of Tourism symbol on the envelope. He'd be sure to ask questions.

It was with eager fingers that, two days later, she ripped open the letter that arrived for her.

'Thinking of seeing some of our own fair State in your holidays?' simpered Miss Peabody, the school secretary.

'It's for a project,' Amanda threw back over her shoulder as she hurried away. She was in no mood to be held up by small talk. Her father's manner over the last few days had heightened her curiosity. It was as if her simple question had put a barrier between them.

'Summer Bay,' she read, 'is a small town of some 3000 residents that nestles picturesquely on the Central Coast of New South Wales. Its appeal lies in its unspoiled and undeveloped beaches. A half-mile long arc of golden sands is lapped by crystal clear, unpolluted waters. These are a delight to both the sun-worshipper and the energetically-inclined. Beautifully formed waves break about a hundred yards from the shore, making this a mecca for surfers. The water closer to the shoreline is tranquil, ensuring large contingents of families on hot days. Infants can be left to toddle safely by the water's edge.'

Amanda closed her eyes. Something about

this last sentence struck a chord. An image was there, trying to emerge from the fog of the past. She could see herself, a nut-brown three-year-old, tapping the top of a sandcastle with her spade. Mummy was laughing, incredibly happy as she had been in the boat. But there was something black, something . . . brooding just outside her field of view. If she could only . . .

Amanda tried to widen the scope of her vision, just as she'd tried a few nights previously. But she couldn't. And then the oddest thought occurred to her. Was it that she couldn't identify the dark presence nearby, or was it that her mind wouldn't let her? She'd read about the subconcious protecting us from things too painful to contemplate. Could this be what was happening? She gave up the task and returned to reading. Perhaps she could jog another memory.

Blah, blah, blah, blah, blah. A lot of boring statistics about local industry, the oyster farm, market gardens etc. And then . . .

'Accommodation in the area is not plentiful, nor is it of a high standard. The local motel has a two-star rating, but is clean and is run by a very friendly staff. The only other accommodation offered is at the Summer Bay Caravan Park run by its genial host, Alf Stewart.'

Stewart. Why did that name mean something? Stewart ... Stewart; Ruth Stewart;
Roo to her friends. Amanda remembered the
name and that, at least for a brief time, she
had been one of those friends.

Amanda rubbed her eyes and stared off into
the distance, working to deal with her puzzlement. The whole affair was becoming more
mysterious by the moment. Why had she
forgotten these things for so long? And why
were they starting to come back to her now?
Other images connected with this girl Roo
were waiting to emerge.

Amanda got the impression of two little girls
crying; herself and another. No, there were
three children there; herself, Roo Stewart
and a boy. They were all of the same age
and colouring. Blond. Someone was yelling,
hitting another person. All three children
were in the dark, terrified as they listened to
the shouts and blows coming from above.
Three children. Herself, Roo Stewart and ...
She searched her mind, but it wouldn't
come. Herself, Roo and a boy. A blond boy.

In a blinding flash, it hit her what she had
to do, for she'd have no peace of mind until
she found out what it all meant. Summer
holidays began in two days. Her father was
going overseas on a business trip and she

was meant to be going with him. What if she should fall ill? She'd have to stay behind. She could say that the family of one of her school friends had offered to look after her. She'd have two weeks to herself. In those two weeks she could answer all the questions by going to Summer Bay, where she felt sure the truth lay.

Suddenly she felt scared, very scared.

What on earth had happened to her when she was three? How could simply trying to remember it send her into a cold sweat? She looked down at her palms and found them glistening. Should she forget all of this and go back to being the carefree kid she was before that totally unexpected flash of memory had started her investigating?

It had all seemed so simple then. It was just a happy image of herself, her father and her laughing mother in a boat, fishing. But somehow she knew it wasn't simple at all. It was very, very complex. She looked down at the brochure in her hand, then up with determination. She would go.

She was past the point of no return.

Matt sat on his surfboard, legs dangling on either side, bobbing up and down as he waited for the next ride. It was a bad day, the water as flat as a mill-pond. The few optimistic surfers who had bothered to wax up their boards were killing time by calling gossip to each other.

'Did you check out that red-head at the Surf Club Dance? What a set of . . .'

'Yeah, yeah Briggsy. We're not blind.'

'Macka reckons he got it away with her out the back.'

'The only thing Macka got it away with was his dirty mind.'

'You reckon he was lyin'?'

'Course he was.'

'Hey Matt. What do you think?'

'What?' Matt was pulled away from his enjoyment of the sunshine and into the conversation.

'D'ya reckon that Briggsy got it on with that red-head at the dance last night?'

'Dunno. Good luck to him if he did.'

He didn't care either way. He just wanted to drift, savouring the sun on his broad, golden-brown back.

'What do you think, Jacko?' He fielded the question to a tall, dark-haired boy on his immediate right, then he switched out.

'What a change,' he thought. 'If anyone had told me four years ago how life'd be now, I'd have told them they were mad.'

It was four years since he'd taken up surfing and here he was, one of the central members of the Summer Bay in-crowd. No one could care less about his father's job any more, and this had helped him come to terms with it himself. All that mattered now was that he was one of the best juvenile surfers on this stretch of the coast. His only rival was his best mate Jacko who, depending on the type of swell, could sometimes get the edge on him in friendly competition.

As his reputation had grown with the years, so too had his body. He had matured into early manhood, his upper torso becoming massive for his age due to the daily exertion of paddling his board out beyond the breakers. He was happier than he had ever been. Even his schoolwork, although not spectacular, was improving with each report card.

'Set coming through.'

Jacko's voice woke him from this review of his good fortune and alerted him to the first swell of the day. He couldn't believe it. From out of nowhere, a huge wave could be seen building up as it moved towards them.

'Whoo!!!'

Matt clenched his fist above his head in a Rocky victory punch.

'Anyone who drops in on me is a dead man,' he called jovially to his mates. Dropping in was the act of cutting off another surfer in the course of a ride by moving your board in front of his.

'It's you and me, Matt,' Jacko called. 'Let's show 'em how it's done.'

As he paddled himself into the rising swell, Matt remembered that day four years ago when he'd watched a surfer and his life had been transformed.

'This one's for you mate, whoever you are,' he thought, as his board started to lift on to the crest of the wave. He tingled with an adrenalin rush, as he looked down the precipice beneath him. This really was a monster, the biggest wave he'd ever ridden. He was tempted to pull out at the last moment, a flash of fear almost convincing him that it was a bone-crusher: a wave that would lift you up and smash you and your board on to the sea-bed. But the sight of Jacko, taking the ride ten yards to his right, galvanized him into action. If Jacko could do it, so could he! His heart leapt into his throat as he committed himself to whatever might come.

His senses snapped into focus as he sped across the surface of the wave. The wind whipped through his hair, the spume flew by, striking him in the face and flecking him like snow, and the wave started to curl above him, the lip reaching down to kiss the surface of the water below.

'Oh wow!' his mind screamed. 'The surfers' dream. I'm going to shoot the tube.'

A perfect crystalline cylinder formed around him as he dashed along the face of the wave, keeping just ahead of a watery obliteration. Behind him, the wave collapsed with a thunderous roar, sending foam shooting past. Ahead, it kept curling, making a perfect O for him to ride through.

'Jacko's back there.'

The brief thought intruded upon his elation; an image of his friend being tumbled around in the death throes of the watery monster. But he didn't have to worry. Jacko would be shaken, but unhurt. Jacko was blessed. Better to focus on the ride.

He could see Stewart's Point in the circle of reality at the end of the tube. He was rushing towards it out of a watery-walled Aladdin's cave, that sparkled with glowing diamonds of refracted sunlight. The roar of the wave's collapse was coming closer and closer behind him. Then it was upon him. He was spat out of the end of the wave, as it finally died its natural death a hundred yards from the shore.

He sank down on his board, the diminishing force of the water carrying him to the sand. He revelled in the thrill of the ride. Then he turned his head to look for Jacko and sighted him just down the beach, grinning and waving.

'You mongrel,' Jacko called. 'I get the Hoover rinse and tumble and you get the ride. Good on you mate!'

Matt flopped on to the sand, letting the wavelets lap over him.

'God's in his heaven and all's right with the world.'

What was that poem Fisher had read out to them last week? Something by Robert Browning.

'Well that Browning bloke must have been thinking about me when he wrote it,' Matt grinned to himself.

Up above and behind him, a bus swept along the main road into town.

Amanda Taylor looked eagerly out of the

window for her first glimpse of the mysterious Summer Bay. Her father was winging his way to Rio via L.A., little dreaming that she was hot on the trail of a long buried secret. She caught a quick glimpse of two surfers on the beach. One stood calling to the other, a blond boy about her own age who was lolling in the shallows. She registered them, then turned away, looking ahead and past the driver for the sign bearing the happy young girl on the air mattress that would welcome her arrival.

Little did she realize that the blond boy she had just sighted was the same one she had played with eleven years before.

And little did Matt realize, as he savoured the triumph of his ride, that the first, and perhaps greatest, love of his life had just arrived in town.

chapter three

At seventeen, Lance and Martin were still the town bozos. But their escapades were tempered by a good-natured enthusiasm which stopped them from fulfilling town prophecy by turning into full-blown delinquents. Living was synonymous with beer, mates and chicks; in that order. They drank more beer than they should; had one mate each, each other; and pulled no chicks whatsoever. But hope sprang eternal.

'Hey Marty, get a load o' her.'

The duo were mooching past the bus stop as Amanda alighted from the bus.

'Fresh flesh.' Martin bayed like a werewolf at full moon. 'Let's check it out, dude.'

'Let's check it out.' Lance tended to echo most of Martin's more pithy phrases.

They sloped across towards Amanda, Martin extracting a comb from the pocket of his skin-tight jeans and flicking it through his greasy locks. The fit of his jeans was not a fashion statement. He'd simply put on weight at an alarming rate, due to his over-consumption of beer.

'Can we help you, beautiful?'

Martin was convinced he was sophistication personified.

'Yeah, can we help?' came the ubiquitous echo from Lance.

Amanda was startled by these examples of local manhood, but she soon sensed that there was no harm in them.

'I'm looking for the Summer Bay Caravan Park. It's run by an Alf Stewart, right?'

'It's run by *the* Alf Stewart, baby. And you are talking to the right dudes. There is nothing about Summer Bay that we don't know. Martin Dibble. That's me. And this dude on my right is Lance.'

'Smart. Lance Smart. Smart's me second name.'

'Smart by name, smart by nature,' Martin chuckled. He was well into cool mode. 'What's your label, baby?'

Amanda stifled a smile. Where did he get his lines from? Old gangster movies?

'Amanda. Amanda . . .'

She hesitated, then committed to the lie.

'. . . Burton.' A second sense told her it might be best to keep her identity to herself until she'd asked a few questions. If there were secrets to be uncovered in Summer Bay, her name might forewarn anyone with things to hide.

'Well, Amanda Burton, give us your bag and we'll walk you to the caravan park.'

Martin sensed her slight hesitation.

'Relax baby. You're lookin' at two gentlemen. Right Lance?'

'Yeah, two gentlemen.' Lance wiped his palm across his nose as if in verification of the fact.

Amanda smiled and handed across her bag. They seemed sweet in a moronic sort of way.

Matt was sauntering up from the beach, his board under his arm, when he caught sight of the unlikely trio. He couldn't believe his eyes. Lance and Martin were with the most beautiful girl he'd ever seen.

'Watch it, Marty.' Lance nudged Martin. Neither had felt comfortable around Matt since his stinking revenge four years ago.

'There's one dude to steer clear of,' Martin warned Amanda. 'He's a real mean customer.'

A little negative P.R. seemed highly advisable. Martin didn't need Matt muscling in on his territory. He already felt that he had staked a claim on Amanda. 'Finders keepers' was his philosophy.

Amanda looked at the subject of their warning. She recognized him as the blond boy she'd seen from the bus window. Her pulse quickened as she met his gaze. At close range he was totally gorgeous; blue eyes that reflected the light from the sea; a sleek, tanned torso that formed a V-shape from his broad shoulders to his slim, tight waist. She had never felt so instantly attracted to a boy. She blushed.

When Amanda's eyes swept over him and she coloured, the naturally modest Matt misinterpreted her look. He felt that he'd been summed up and dismissed. The beautiful girl had flushed in anger; anger, because she had read his thoughts. She was signalling 'back off'. Matt lowered his gaze and walked past.

'He's not interested,' Amanda thought. 'Why would he be? He must have every girl in town chasing him.'

'Yeah, that's right. Rack off,' Martin mumbled after Matt.

'If he gives you any trouble, let us know,' he added in Amanda's direction. 'He knows not to mess with us.'

'. . . not to mess with us.' Many of Lance's echoes made no grammatical sense at all.

'There you go.' Martin pointed up ahead. 'Summer Bay Caravan Park.'

It was with difficulty that Amanda shook off the eager pair. Only by promising to seek them out and join them for a milkshake, could she finally walk up the caravan park's winding driveway alone. Her nervousness temporarily drove thoughts of Matt from her mind.

Alf Stewart's daughter, Roo, was definitely the little girl who'd been with her in the dark all those years ago. Would she remember her? Would she recall who had been shouting and fighting that night? Would she know who struck the blows that Amanda had remembered hearing? Could she fill in any of the gaps?

Perhaps, if Roo didn't remember, her father or mother would be able to supply the answers.

Amanda knocked at the door of the large two-storey house that dominated the caravan park. No answer. She knocked again, louder.

'Can I help you, lovey?'

A plump, jovial-looking woman called to her from the door of a garishly painted wagon. The lettering on the side announced that fortunes were told within.

'I'm Floss. You lookin' for a van?'

'Yes. Yes, I am.'

'I may as well stay here,' Amanda thought. 'It looks like it could be different. Fun.'

Floss waddled over.

'Alf and Roo aren't home right now. School holidays. He's taken her up to the city to visit her Aunty Morag. I'm lookin' after the vans.'

Amanda's heart sank. Why had she assumed that Roo would be here? But Floss offered immediate hope.

'They've only gone for the weekend. They'll be back Monday, maybe even earlier. Holiday season's too busy for Alf to be away long. Come on in.'

Floss led the way into a large and homely

living room, with a small kitchen annexe. She prattled on as she collected a key to one of the vans, led Amanda outside and settled her into Number 15.

'It's our deluxe suite.' Floss smiled and winked. 'Still, it's cheap. If there's anything you want, give a hoi. Nev and me are just across the way. The beach is down that path marked Beach. Of course it is. Listen to me prattlin' on. Any groceries or anythin' like that you can get at Ailsa Hogan's. It's in the main drag.'

'I saw it when I got off the bus.'

'Ailsa's new to town too. She seems real nice. City lass like yourself.'

Amanda sensed that Floss was probing with this last statement, trying to find out where Amanda was from. So she supplied a potted history, albeit a false one, to stop any further subtle or not so subtle questioning.

The gossip vine in Summer Bay was such that Matt heard it all over dinner.

'Apparently some pretty city girl's moved in to one of the vans at Alf's,' Matt's mother said as she dished up the vegetables. 'Floss says she's only in her teens and there's no sign of any parents. Shocking, isn't it? Letting a young girl go off on her own like that? What can her family be thinking of?'

Matt's father smiled and winked at Matt. He enjoyed teasing his wife.

'Don't tell me Celia Stewart's converted you into a do-gooder, Dawn, stickin' your nose into other people's business?'

'I was only saying, Gary, would you like Matt wandering off on his own? And he's a boy.'

'What does she look like?' Matt asked, full of curiosity.

He suspected this must be the girl he'd seen with Lance and Martin. They were heading in the direction of the caravan park and she'd had a bag.

'Why are you so interested?' Dawn asked.

Matt's dad laughed at the look of unease on his wife's face.

'Don't worry, mum. Matt's not gonna get up to no good.'

Matt blushed, annoyed at the obvious suspicion behind his mother's manner.

'What do you think I'm going to do, rush over there and race her off?'

'You watch your tongue, young man,' Dawn snapped. 'There's no need to be crude.'

'I was just curious. You don't have to make a big deal about it.'

'I wasn't.'

Silence descended. There were often differences of opinion in the Wilson household, but none of them were serious. This was a home full of love.

Dawn realized it was up to her to elaborate on what she'd meant.

'A young girl like that, on her own ... there's no saying what type she might be. Boys have got themselves into trouble with wild young things before now.'

'If it's the girl I think it is, she didn't look wild at all. She looked really ... classy.' Matt smiled at the memory of her beauty. 'So tell us. What do you know about her?'

Dawn took a deep breath, preparing to launch into a gossip session. She blushed as she saw her husband and son stifling affectionate laughter.

'What?'

'Nothing.'

'Don't laugh at me.'

'It's just you, Mum. You love a good gossip, don't you?'

Dawn ruffled her son's hair, as if to say 'get away with you'. Harmony was fully restored.

'She's very pretty apparently. Blonde. Looks about seventeen, Floss says, but she's sure she's younger. She said she wanted to get away somewhere different for the holidays, so she took out a map and stuck a pin into it. She hit Summer Bay.'

'Still doesn't explain why her parents aren't with her,' Gary interjected.

'She told Floss that they trust her. It's more than I'd do with a pretty young daughter. Still, Floss and Nev are going to keep an eye on her. One thing that puzzled Floss though, the girl seemed real curious about Alf and Roo; especially Roo. You know how Floss is, with her second sight and all. She reckons there's definitely more to it than meets the eye. She's convinced the girl's down here with a purpose.'

'Mumbo jumbo,' laughed Gary.

'Don't you be so sure. Remember when I lost that bracelet of mine? Floss told me exactly where it was.'

'Lucky guess.' Dealing in the disposal of rubbish all day had hardened Gary into the ultimate pragmatist. Matt did not take after him. He'd seen other examples of Floss McPhee's powers and if Floss said this girl was hiding something then she was. But what? The girl suddenly became even more intriguing.

'Amanda Burton's her name.' Dawn finally supplied the most important piece of information.

'Amanda. What a fantastic name,' Matt thought, as he wandered along the road into town half an hour later. By hook or by crook, he'd get to talk to her. Just the thought of it made him feel excited.

He walked past Hogan's Store, deep in thought. If he had glanced to the right, through the open doorway of the shop, he would have seen the subject of his reverie in conversation with Ailsa.

Ring, ring!

A light pierced the gloom in front of him, a warning bell announcing the approach of a bike. He could tell that tone anywhere. Celia. That was all he needed. Maybe she wouldn't recognize him in the dark.

'Is that you, Matthew?'

His heart sank, as she drew level with him. Not another one of her lectures.

'Yes, Miss Stewart.'

'Shouldn't you be home studying?'

'It's school holidays, Miss Stewart.'

'A good time to catch up. Year Ten is very important.'

'Here we go,' thought Matt.

To his great surprise Celia sailed right on by, calling back a farewell and another encouragement to study as she went. Clearly she had other fish to fry.

'Pity the poor person, whoever it is,' Matt thought, as he whistled off cheerily into the night.

'Ailsa, my dear. Have you heard? There's a homeless waif staying at the caravan park.'

Celia was in full flight as she bustled into the store. She carried her shopping basket, as a covering excuse for her arrival. She had been sitting at home when she'd been seized with the desire to chat. Calls to her two partners-in-gossip, Betty Fallwell and Doris Peters, had borne no fruit. Clearly they were both out. Together? And without her? She'd take them to task about that tomorrow. But for now?

So she had taken to her bike and headed for the store. One thing about Ailsa, she was a guaranteed listener. She had to be on duty until nine o'clock, which was closing time.

'Celia . . .' Ailsa tried to head her off at the pass, for Celia had not seen Amanda at the shelves, choosing her groceries.

'A pretty little thing, I'm told. Do you think she could be a runaway? It seems very strange to me, a girl of her age arriving in town alone. Perhaps Bob Barnett should be informed.'

'Celia . . .'

'I know what you're going to say, Ailsa, and my answer is no. I cannot turn my back on the situation. It is my duty as a Christian woman to worry about those less fortunate than myself. Who knows what sort of moral danger this young lass is exposed to, even as we speak? Doris saw her with Martin Dibble and Lance Smart. I shudder to think of her at the mercy of those two hooligans.'

'CELIA!!!'

Ailsa's more forceful interruption stopped her dead in her tracks.

'I'd like you to meet Amanda Burton. Amanda, this is Celia Stewart. As I'm sure you've gathered, Celia is our local angel of mercy.'

'There's no need to tease, Ailsa dear.'

Celia blushed, in some degree of confusion, as she turned to find Amanda behind her.

'What will the young girl think of me?' she thought.

But the charming smile that she encountered set her completely at ease and allayed any suspicions she might have had about Amanda's moral fibre.

'I'm very pleased to meet you, Miss Stewart. Thank you for taking the time to concern yourself with my welfare.'

'What a charming girl,' Celia thought. Floss McPhee was clearly wrong, as usual. This was an open and smiling young face.

Amanda's brain was racing. Stewart? Could this woman be related to Alf Stewart? If she was, she was no doubt around eleven years ago, and her gossipy type stored up the most trivial memories for years. Amanda sensed that she could well benefit from a talk with Celia.

'I'm just about to walk home to my caravan. If you're going in that direction, Miss Stewart, I'd appreciate the company.'

Celia was used to people making excuses to avoid her. Very rarely did anyone actually encourage her. And here was this mine of gossip-fodder laying herself open to subtle probing. It was too good to be true. This would teach Betty and Doris to go off to the pictures or wherever and exclude her from their outing. Only if they asked very nicely would she divulge any findings she might make; and perhaps not even then.

'Your shopping, Celia?' Ailsa called after her dryly, as the gossip escorted Amanda from the shop.

'I shall do it tomorrow,' Celia threw back. 'I'm sure Amanda is in a hurry to get home. Now dear, you must tell me all about yourself.'

Ailsa smiled, as the sound of Celia's chatter faded into the night. There was no accounting for this mystery girl's taste in companions.

It took a good half of the journey for Amanda to get a word in edgewise. When she finally did, she went straight to the heart of the matter. But with subtlety. She made her tone as casual as possible.

'I heard about Summer Bay through a friend of mine. She came down with her parents when she was little. She was only about three, I think.'

'Dear me, it must have made a strong impression on her if she can still remember,' Celia twittered. 'But why should I be surprised? I find Summer Bay to be God's little acre. Why shouldn't others?'

'Perhaps you can remember my friend's family?'

'Oh I doubt it dear. Is she your age?'

'Yes.'

'Dear me then. Three from . . .?'

Celia prided herself on this subtle move to extract Amanda's actual age.

'Fourteen.'

'Three from fourteen. Eleven years ago. Even my memory isn't that good.'

Celia's thoughts darkened. Only fourteen. This wasn't good enough. A young girl of her age alone. Where were her parents? This could well be a case for Bob after all.

'The family's name was Taylor,' Amanda persevered. 'Bernard and Daphne Taylor. And my friend's name's Amanda too.'

'Taylor? Daphne Taylor? Now that name rings a bell.'

'Yes?' Amanda's eyes glowed. 'My friend said she used to play with Alf Stewart's daughter Ruth and a little blond boy. Are you related to Ruth?'

'She's my niece.'

'Perhaps you remember her playing with

my friend then? Or even the entire family being around the caravan park?'

'Daphne Taylor. It definitely rings some sort of bell, but I can't think why. Bernard and Daphne Taylor . . .'

For a moment it looked as if the clouds were about to clear. But then she shook her head.

'No. No, it won't come. Anyway, it's not important, is it? What's important is that you have a wonderful time whilst you're here and that you are looked after in a manner that your parents would no doubt wish for. Now, I have a suggestion. We have an extra bedroom at home. I live with my mother and father. They're in their sixties, but they're very young at heart. I think you would enjoy staying with us. Please? It would put my mind at rest. One reads such dreadful things in the newspapers.'

'That's very nice of you, Miss Stewart, but I'm quite safe. Floss and Neville are just next door and they're keeping an eye on me.'

'What have I started here?' she thought.

'My friend asked me to look up the little boy she played with when she was here and say hi,' she continued. 'She can't even remember his name. Can you think who he might be?'

53

'Now, are you positive about not taking up my offer?' Celia pressed.

'Absolutely, Miss Stewart. The boy?'

'Ah, well. It's still there if you change your mind. He was fair-haired, you say?'

'Yes.'

'And he used to play with Ruth when she was three?'

'Yes.'

Celia thought. Of course. There was only one person it could be.

The next morning, as Matt prepared to paddle out to catch his first wave of the day, his pulse started to race. There, coming down the beach was the girl he'd dreamt about all last night. Amanda.

He had to talk to her. What could he say without making a complete fool of himself? He played various lines through in his head, discarding them all as either obvious, corny, sleazy or just plain dumb. There was nothing for it, he thought. Just smile as she goes by and talk to her next time. It'd seem less desperate that way.

So he was completely taken by surprise when

she walked straight up to him and made the running herself.

'Hi, I'm Amanda. Could we have a talk?'

chapter four

Celia stirred in her sleep and looked at the bedside clock. Ten past seven. Time to get up and put on the kettle. She leapt from the bed and did five knee bends and took ten deep breaths. The body is the temple of the Lord, was her motto. It needed to be tended as much as the mind.

Daphne Taylor. The name and the nagging question hit her once more. Who was Daphne Taylor? It had tormented her as she tossed and turned in the early hours of the morning. Something lurked at the back of her mind, but she couldn't put her finger on it.

Then, suddenly, it came. Of course. Daphne Taylor. Why had it taken her so long to remember? Such a shocking story. Perhaps that was why. It was the sort of thing you wanted to block out. She must tell Amanda. But no. On second thoughts, it was none of the girl's affair. It wasn't as if she was related to the Taylors; she was just a friend of their daughter's. And she was so young. Certain things were not fit for the ears of a fourteen-year-old.

Even a gossip like Celia had some scruples.

Matt thought he must be dreaming. He pinched himself underneath the table. No. He was still there. This was real, and reality had never felt so good. He could feel the envious glances of the guys walking past. He and Amanda sat at an umbrella-covered table outside Ailsa's store. She licked an ice-cream cone as they talked. He could sit there watching her all day.

'Sorry?'

She had asked him a question and he'd been too busy counting his blessings to listen. What would she think? He could kick himself.

'I asked if you remember a girl called Amanda Taylor. She's a friend of mine. She said she used to play with you about eleven years ago.'

'Eleven years?'

'Yeah.'

'I was only three then. No way I'd remember.'

'She said something about you and her and a girl called Roo Stewart sitting in the dark, hearing people arguing. Then there was the sound of someone or something being hit. Does that ring a bell?'

Matt laughed.

'You've got to be kidding. You just don't remember stuff from that far back.'

'Right.' Amanda couldn't hide her disappointment.

'Why? Is it important?'

'No, of course not.'

Amanda's reply was just that bit too sharp to be convincing.

'Do you really have a friend called Amanda? Or are you asking for yourself?'

She was thrown by his seeing through her.

'I'm not a member of the Celia Stewart club. Anything you tell me stops here,' he added.

Amanda looked at him. She needed so desperately to confide in someone, to share her feelings. But was Matt the right person? Could she trust him? She studied his handsome, open face for a few more moments and decided that she could.

'Yeah, it's me.'

'So what's your real name? Burton or Taylor?'

'Taylor. Amanda Taylor.'

'And that's why you're here? You want to know about something that happened when you were three?'

'Yeah.'

'Why?'

Amanda gave him a quick version of what she'd been through. She told him of her sudden flashes of memory, of her puzzlement at her father's denials, of her growing sense that something very important was being kept from her and of the feeling that the entire future of her relationship with her father rested upon getting answers to her questions.

And as she talked, she felt herself warming to this handsome guy across the table. She sensed that he actually cared what happened to her.

'If Celia doesn't know anything, no one does,' Matt said, when she had told him everything, including last night's chat with the town gossip. "Specially as it's something that happened to Roo. She knows everything that goes on in her family.'

Suddenly he had an inspiration.

'Come on.'

He took her hand and dragged her to her feet.

'Where to?'

'The caravan park. There's someone there who's amazing.'

She nearly laughed when he told her what he had in mind. Consult a fortune-teller? Floss was very sweet, but to take her carry-on seriously? Maybe she was wrong about Matt? Anyone who could believe in that sort of stuff . . .

Despite her objections, she found herself sitting across the table from the old woman. Neville was winding fishing tackle at the other end of the tiny van and Matt hovered at her right shoulder. With the four of them crammed in, there wasn't much room to move.

'You've got to take this seriously, lovey, or it won't work.'

'I told her you're good Floss,' Matt chimed in.

'Thanks for the P.R., lovey. Now, why don't you stop jumpin' about and sit next to Nev.

I can't concentrate if there are distractions. Ball or cards, lovey?'

'Sorry?' asked Amanda.

'The crystal ball or the tarot? I prefer the cards myself.'

'Whatever.' It was all Amanda could do not to laugh.

Floss shuffled the cards, then gave them to Amanda to complete the process. Then she had the girl place them out. Once this was done, she considered the pattern.

'You're on a quest. You're looking for answers.'

For a moment, Amanda was impressed. Then she snorted to herself. That was a pretty fair guess for the old girl to make. Otherwise, why would she be asking for a reading in the first place?

'I see three little kiddies. It's dark. They're scared.'

Amanda felt goose bumps from her head to her feet. Then she searched for a rational explanation. Had Matt and Floss been alone together at any time since they arrived? Could he have told her this? Had she said anything to Floss herself that could have led the old fake to surmise as much? She racked her brain. The answer was no to all three questions. Then how on earth could Floss know?

Nev nodded sagely. 'She can be pretty clever, the old girl can. Don't ask me how she does it.'

'Shh, Nev,' Floss snapped gently as she turned her attention back to the cards.

'There's a fourth child.'

'No, there were only three.'

'There's definitely four kiddies here. You say only three?'

'Yes.' Maybe she's not so good after all, Amanda thought. Maybe the first bit was just a fluke.

Floss frowned. She looked at the cards as if into a deep well. Suddenly her frown was overlaid by a look of alarm. Before Amanda knew what was happening, Floss had reached forward and shuffled the pattern out of existence.

'I'm a silly old fool who should know better. I'm sorry, lovey, I deserve a good tickin' off for teasin' you. A couple of young kids like yourselves; you should be out on the beach soakin' up the sun. You don't wanna be in here, listenin' to an old fraud like me. Off you go and enjoy yourselves.'

Despite Matt's protests, they found themselves outside the caravan with the door shut in their faces.

'The kids in the dark; it was a fluke.'

Amanda wanted to convince herself. She felt rattled by Floss's barely-covered alarm.

'I don't know,' Matt replied, trying to fathom out Floss's behaviour.

'She said four kids,' Amanda continued. 'There *were* only three that night. I know it. As soon as Floss realized she'd made a mistake she decided not to go on. That's what it was. She realized she was making a fool of herself. Come on. I need a swim.'

She ran ahead of him. Matt followed thoughtfully, glancing back at the dilapidated old carnival wagon.

Inside, Floss sat on the edge of the bed.

'What is it, lovey?' Nev asked, concerned by her pallor.

'There's been death and there will be death. Death in Summer Bay. Hold me, lovey. Sometimes I hate the power. I really do. That poor little mite should get away from here.'

Neville rocked her gently, concerned by her genuine distress.

*

Amanda dived into the pounding waves, trying to wash away her unease. She swam with strong strokes out through and past the breakers. Then she waited for a strong swell and bodysurfed in.

Matt watched from where he stood knee-deep in the shallows. He didn't know what to make of Amanda. He had the feeling that an involvement with her could bring a lot of complications. But this disquiet was replaced by admiration, as she expertly rode the wave towards him.

She had the lines and grace of the dolphins that surfed Summer Bay in schools each winter. Her tanned, lithe body became one with the wave, her wet hair flew out behind her and her face lifted back and clear of the foam as she let out a happy cry. Then the wave folded over her and she was lost in the tumble wash. As she found her feet and rose out of the water, flicking her hair from her face in one smooth motion, Matt knew that he had no choice. Complications or not, he had to keep seeing this dream come true.

'That was fantastic!' she called exuberantly.

'Feel better now?'

'Absolutely. Come on. Let's catch some more.'

She started to swim out in search of another wave. This was exactly what she needed. The exhilaration of the ride to take her mind off that obsession which had brought her here; the obsession to break through the barrier across her memory; the obsession to remember that long-vanished summer.

'Hang on a minute. Have you ever tried the real thing?'

Matt's words brought Amanda to a halt.

'I hope you don't mean what I think you mean.'

Matt laughed and blushed at her mis-understanding.

'Not that. What do you take me for? I meant surfing. Real surfing. On a board. Have you ever tried it?'

'I know that's what you meant. I just wanted to see you blush.'

Matt met her smile and returned it. Their eyes locked.

'God,' he thought. 'It's like in all those slushy movies. Looking into her eyes . . . it really is like falling into a pool or something.'

'He's so cute,' Amanda thought in her turn. 'And so nice. I should forget why I came here. Drop all that and just enjoy being with him.'

Each recognized the other's attraction, each knew that something important was happening, each knew that this was a feeling they had not experienced before.

'Maybe this is that love-at-first-sight stuff they talk about,' thought Matt. But, showing his father's pragmatic streak, he went on to consider further. 'Except it's not first sight, it's sort of like . . . instant attraction after thinking for a bit. Still, that's just as romantic.'

'All the guys in the city are so smooth. He's so open, so different. I really want to get to know him well,' Amanda thought in her turn.

The silence between them hung in the air, as they wrestled with their feelings. Matt, feeling awkward, finally broke it.

'So *have* you ever done the real thing?'

'No, but I'd love to. Are you going to teach me?'

'Too right I am. Wait here. I'll get my board.'

Matt had dropped it off at home on the way over to the caravan park. He hurried up the beach, not wanting to be away from Amanda any longer than was necessary. He had a strange feeling that she would disappear if he didn't hurry back.

'This is crazy,' he thought. 'I hardly know her and I'm worrying about never seeing her again.'

Amanda watched his broad back as he ran up the sandy path to the roadway and disappeared from view.

'Come back quickly,' she thought. 'I don't want to start thinking about Floss's reading again.'

Then it suddenly occurred to her that this wasn't the only reason she wanted him to hurry. She wanted him back for himself.

'What is this?' she thought. 'I've only just met him and I'll probably never see him again once I leave Summer Bay. Why am I feeling like this?'

But somehow, already, she knew that she would keep in touch with him. She wouldn't be able not to. Dreamily, she pushed the sand at her feet into a mound. Then she started to mould it, patting and pinching battlements and turrets into being. A castle took shape as her hands expertly worked the wet sand.

Suddenly she froze. She stared at the shape in front of her. Without thinking, she had sculpted the castle of her memories, the castle that had been made as she played on the beach eleven years ago. As she looked at it, as congealed grains fell away and rolled down its sides, so the walls of her memory block started to crumble.

It hit her that this was the exact spot where she had played all those years ago. She closed her eyes and could see the image of herself and Mummy, making the castle. Once again she knew that if she turned her head in the memory, a black and threatening vision would burst upon her from her left-hand side. Better to turn to the right then. There was Daddy, laughing and smiling too. How silly. For a moment she had feared that he was the ominous presence brooding so close, yet to the other side of her. Did she dare face the truth? She had to.

Very slowly, in her mind's eye, she turned her head. Back into the centre, away from Daddy. Keep going, sweeping past Mummy. Coming around fully to the left. She was facing blackness; that's all it was. A blank, dark hole in the vibrant colour of the rest of the memory. And somewhere in that darkness was a person?

Suddenly tears welled in her eyes. She couldn't help herself. She started to sob. For she realized that, at that point in time, she had truly loved the person in the black hole of forgetfulness. How and when had that love turned to terror? How and when had fear woven a black cloud of forgetfulness and blocked this person from her life?

The tears rolled down Amanda's face, as she snapped her eyes open, forcing a return to the present. It was too painful to stay back in the past; too painful to face the questions.

'Hey Marty, she's cryin'.'

'Eh, right mate. She is.'

Lance and Martin shuffled down the beach towards Amanda. Martin felt heartened. A damsel in distress. A cool dude like himself would earn mega-gratitude if he could comfort her. And who knew where that gratitude might lead.

'Get lost, eh Lance.'

'How come?'

'Cos two's sexy and three's a drag, right? I wanna crack on to her.' Martin despaired. His friend could be so slow sometimes.

'Yeah, but what about me, Marty?'

'Go and find your own chick.'

'I saw her same time as you did. How come she's yours?'

Martin sensed rebellion and he didn't like it.

'Cos I say so. Now scram, dork-brain. Go over to the convent school at Yabbie Creek. There's bulk chicks there.'

'Yeah, but I don't want them. I want Amanda.'

Martin could have throttled him. His big chance and Lance was going to ruin it by his refusal to disappear. There was only so much cool that you could muster in a crowd. The art of the true con was a one-on-one experience.

Amanda turned.

'Hi.' She managed a sad smile. 'If you don't mind, I'd rather be alone.'

'Too late to get rid of Lance,' Martin thought. 'I'll just have to wing it.'

'That's what you think now,' he began smoothly, starting to lower himself on to the sand beside her. 'But I'm a guy who's used to listenin' to problems. See this shoulder? I have to wring m' shirt out sometimes. Cryin', you see. Chicks cryin' on it. You've got a problem, go to Marty Dibble; that's what they all say 'round here.'

'Do they?' Lance couldn't remember anyone ever having said that.

'Shut up and rack off,' Martin hissed at Lance from the side of his mouth. 'Course they do.'

He swung his oily grin back towards Amanda. He reached out and wiped a tear from her cheek, admiring his own technique as he did so.

'Just lay your head down there, baby, and let it all hang out.'

He went to put his arm around Amanda, as a prelude to guiding her head on to his broad and masculine shoulder. But a harsh voice called out:

'Leave her alone, Dibble. You too, Smart. Rack off before I make you both do an ostrich impression.'

Amanda wiped the tears from her cheeks and turned, surprised by this side of Matt. He came striding down the beach, like a knight in shining armour.

Martin stood, sidling up to Lance for support. Despite the fact that Matt was two years younger than them, he had matured into a powerful young man. Martin would prefer to avoid violence. Besides, Matt's mates in the surf club were all bruisers.

'Don't get your yo-yos in a knot,' Martin called. 'Just talkin' to her. She was upset, right? Nothin' wrong with a bloke comfortin' a lady.'

'There is when he uses it as an excuse for a grope. So rack off. Both of you!'

Lance jumped, as Matt barked the last command. Like all bullies, this deadly duo turned coward at the drop of a hat. Lance immediately took to his heels, attempting to look casual.

'Reckon I will go and check out those chicks at Yabbie Creek after all, Marty.'

'That'll teach a bloke to try and do the right thing, mate. Sheilas! They're not worth it, I reckon.'

Martin followed his friend down the beach, calling back to Amanda when he had put enough distance between himself and the aggressive Matt.

'You want to take me up on m' offer, I'm always around. Remember . . .'

He patted his shoulder as if to indicate that a world of comfort could be found by nestling against it.

'And remember what I told you yesterday. Watch him.'

He quickened his pace, just in case Matt took umbrage at his final comment.

'I can look after myself you know,' Amanda smiled up at Matt.

He could see that she had indeed been crying. He stared down the beach angrily towards the departing drongoes.

'What did they say?'

'Nothing. It wasn't them. In fact, if anything, Martin made me laugh again. He's so bad at being Mr Smooth. I feel sorry for him.'

'Don't waste your time,' said Matt. 'He's the town joke; him and Lance together.'

'How come you're like that about them? It's not just that they were bothering me, surely?'

'They used to rag me when I was little. Made m' life miserable. Until I stood up to them.'

'What did they rag you about?'

'About my Dad. Because he's a . . .'

For the first time in years he hesitated to tell someone about his father's profession. He'd got over that hang-up the day he rode his first wave. But with Amanda . . . She was a classy girl. Maybe his family background would turn her off.

'Because he's a what?' she asked.

Suddenly Matt hated himself. He was not going to go back to being the scared little kid, ashamed of the fine, good man who was his father. If Amanda was snob enough to let the truth affect her, well . . . she wasn't the girl he thought she was.

'My Dad's a garbage man. They used to tease me about it.'

'Don't sound so defensive.' Amanda smiled gently. She sensed what was going through his mind. 'It doesn't matter to me what your Dad does.'

'It doesn't?'

'Of course not. What sort of a snob do you think I am?'

She returned his smile, then leapt to her feet and held out her hand.

'I thought you were going to teach me to surf. Come on.'

Matt took the offered hand got up and hurried into the surf with her, his board under his other arm.

From the top of the sand dunes, Lance and Martin watched the pair cavorting.

'It's not fair,' mumbled Martin. 'What's he got that I haven't?',

'A surfboard, eh?' This was the only advantage Lance could possibly imagine Matt having over his mate. 'Maybe she's into surfies.'

Martin shook his head, incredulous.

'There's no tellin' with some chicks, is there? Would 'a' thought a chick like her'd have more taste. Ah well.'

He emitted a philosophical sigh.

'Let's go over to Yabbie Creek, eh?'

'Too right,' Lance chuckled enthusiastically. 'Them Yabbie Creek convent chicks are better 'n her any day.'

'Yeah,' sneered Martin, unconvinced.

They turned their backs on the happy couple, just as Amanda stood for the first time on the board.

'You're a natural,' Matt laughed, as she came tumbling down into his arms.

Floss walked across the caravan park towards the house. She hoped that what she was doing was right, but she couldn't turn her back on what she had seen. Someone close to Amanda had already died here, and Amanda would too. Unless . . .

The cards were a warning. What they predicted didn't have to come true. If Amanda left Summer Bay and never came back, what Floss had seen would never happen.

She let herself into the house and picked up the phone. She looked at the number in her hand, as she dialled. She had not liked going through Amanda's things, but it was for the girl's own good. She had found her name, address and phone number. Amanda Taylor. Floss wondered why she had lied and called herself Amanda Burton. Perhaps she was a runaway as Celia had suggested.

'Hello, Taylor residence.'

A woman's voice came down the line.

'Hello. I was wondering if Mr or Mrs Taylor were there?'

'Mr Taylor is overseas. Mrs Taylor died a year ago. I'm the housekeeper. Can I help you?'

'Could I speak to Amanda then?' asked Floss. Maybe the woman would say something that would indicate where they thought Amanda was.

'She's away for the holidays, visiting a friend.'

'So she did lie,' thought Floss.

'I see. I was wondering, would it be possible for you to pass a message on to Mr Taylor? It's very important.'

'Certainly.'

'Could you tell him that Amanda isn't where he thinks she is? She's in a place called Summer Bay, on her own. Tell him she's staying at the caravan park. Thank you.'

'Who is this?' The housekeeper was puzzled by the mysterious call. 'You must be mistaken.'

'It doesn't matter who I am. And I'm not wrong. I'm worried about Amanda. Please let Mr Taylor know, and tell him that the sooner he gets Amanda away from here the better. This is very important. You must tell him. Thank you.'

Floss hung up, hearing the questioning voice of the housekeeper coming from the receiver as she lowered it. She felt terrible. She had interfered, she had betrayed the girl. But she knew that it was for the best. Still, she couldn't suppress her guilt.

So later, when she saw Amanda and Matt

coming happily into the caravan park from the direction of the beach, she scurried into her van and closed the door. She couldn't face the kids. For, even though she may have saved Amanda's life, she felt another premonition: that she had opened the flood-gates to a world of heartache for both young-sters.

chapter five

The The First Class cabin on Qantas Flight 4 from Los Angeles to Sydney was full, but Bernard Taylor was oblivious to the other passengers. He sat, slumped in his chair, staring at the back of the seat in front of him. The intensity of his gaze made it appear as if there were some inscrutable hieroglyphics inscribed upon it, which Bernard was trying to decipher. But it was the ghosts of the past that claimed his attention, ghosts that only he could see.

He could envisage the inside of the caravan, as if it were yesterday. He could see the pale and limp body of the child before him. He could see himself, desperately beating and pounding the tiny frame. He could hear his wife's screams. And then . . .

He broke away from the thought. It was too threatening. But his mind was finally drawn back by its magnetic pull.

He saw the accusing gaze of his three-year-old daughter, as she stood in the doorway of the caravan, surveying the scene. Then he watched her face make the journey from mystification, to awareness, to horror, as her child's mind grappled with the sight before her.

'Stop hurting her, Daddy. Stop hurting her.'

And his wife's hysterical sobbing in counterpoint.

'She's dead. Oh my God, Bernard, she's dead.'

'A drink, sir?'

The bland voice and Barbie Doll face of the hostess intruded into the world of his past.

'No, thank you,' he managed in reply.

'Can I get you anything at all? You look rather pale.'

'I'm fine. Thank you.'

Bernard buried himself in the *Los Angeles Times*, the better to block out his surroundings. He sensed his neighbour preparing to engage in mid-air camaraderie. Being up to neither small talk nor diplomacy, he knew he would end up being rude if he didn't immediately discourage any conversational overtures. He lapsed back into his thoughts.

He had not been able to believe his ears when he'd received the call.

'It was the oddest message, sir, I thought it must have been a prank,' said the house-keeper. 'So I called Mr and Mrs Morton. Not only is Amanda not ill, as she told us, but she's not staying with them. They had no idea she was even supposed to be. She's obviously lied to you sir, so she could go to this . . . Summer Bay, wherever it might be.'

'I know where it is, Mrs Thompson,' he'd replied mechanically. He'd felt like he was dying inside. 'I'll catch the first flight home. Do nothing until I get there.'

'But shouldn't the police . . .?'

'NOTHING, do you hear? This is between me and Amanda, no one else.'

He had lived with the terrible secret for so many years. It had eaten away at his mar-riage, until it existed in name only. Appear-ances had been kept up for Amanda's sake.

It had also haunted his relationship with his daughter, for he lived with the constant fear that she would remember. The doctors had warned that her memory could return at any time. It might take days, they said; or weeks, or years. On the other hand, it might never happen. Often, in such cases of hysterical amnesia in children, the memories started to come with the advent of puberty. He had been on tenterhooks as Amanda entered her thirteenth and fourteenth years.

Then the dreaded question came. What and where was Summer Bay? A chink had appeared in the wall surrounding her memory, a wall he had hoped would remain intact for her entire life. He couldn't bear the thought of losing her, the one person he loved in the entire world, yet the truth would no doubt take her from him.

To think that she was there now, in Summer Bay, asking questions. She may already have the answers she was seeking. Would he arrive to find her eyes full of hatred, loathing and accusation?

'No!'

He started, aware that his horror at the thought had made him call out. He could sense the eyes turned in his direction from the seat beside him. He lowered the paper and forced a smile.

'I just checked the market. My shares all took a tumble today.'

The jowly face looking back at him, broke into a relieved smile of identification. Better to have an anxious fellow businessman next to you than a nutter who talked to himself for no reason.

'It's not getting any easier to make a buck these days, is it?' Bernard's travelling companion sympathized, seizing the chance to talk.

Bernard watched the folds of fat quiver around the man's chin, as he chattered on about his own recent business reverses.

'If only he knew,' thought Bernard. 'He'd soon shut up if he knew me for what I am. Then he wouldn't even want to sit next to me. And who would blame him?'

Amanda looked through the clothes she had brought with her and wanted to kick herself. Why hadn't she considered the possibility that she would have to dress up for a date? There was nothing here that was right. It was all casual day wear; jeans, T-shirts, blouses, sneakers. Not that she imagined that Matt would take her anywhere particularly up-market. But she wanted to make an effort. She wanted him to be impressed when he arrived to pick her up.

Matt was having his own similar headaches.

'What'll I do Mum? This stuff's so daggy.'

Dawn Wilson smiled to herself. Her little boy was growing up.

'You've got a perfectly nice sports jacket and those tan slacks go well with it. I'm sure your young lady'll be really impressed.'

'You don't understand though. She's . . . incredible.'

'If she's that special, she'll understand that fourteen-year-old boys in Summer Bay don't go out lookin' like somethin' out of a fashion magazine. Your jacket and your slacks . . . they're fine.'

'That's a nice jacket,' Amanda said, as Matt entered the caravan.

'You really think so?' He preened. Good old Mum, she was always right.

'Of course,' Amanda assured him. 'Sorry I look so awful though. It's the best I brought with me.'

She had worked miracles with jeans, a T-shirt and a scarf, wrapping the scarf around her waist, where it hung enticingly over her hips and set off the simple outfit to perfection.

'You look great.'

'You're only saying that,' she blushed. Why did he have the power to make her feel wonderful with a simple compliment?'

'No, really, I mean it. The other guys are going to hate me.'

'Why?' She knew what he was implying, but she wanted to hear him say it.

Matt met her eyes with a deep and penetrating gaze.

'Because you're the most beautiful girl who's ever been in Summer Bay.'

She didn't believe it for a moment, but she wanted to think he genuinely thought so. Beauty is in the eye of the beholder, they say, and it was important to her that in Matt's eyes she was special.

Suddenly she felt an overwhelming desire to kiss him. She had to get him out of there. What would he think of her if she succumbed to it?

'I'd love to kiss her,' thought Matt. 'She'd probably slap my face.'

'Let's go,' Amanda smiled.

She moved out past him.

'Maybe she could sense what I wanted,' worried Matt. 'She'll probably think I try it on with all the girls.'

'I hope he couldn't tell what I was thinking,' thought Amanda. 'He'll assume I come on

to guys all the time. I really want him to
realize this is different.'

These uncertainties were pushed out of their
heads as the night progressed and they
relaxed with each other. Amanda found herself having one of the best times she'd ever
had. They went to the Surf Club, where a
number of local parents had set up a coffee
shop and dance floor for the teenagers. She
met Matt's friends and was pleased to see
how popular he was. There was a relaxed
feeling to the evening that made it stand
out from her usual nights on the town.
This had it all over the stuffy, pretentious
atmosphere of private school dances and
glitzy discos.

'Where did you find her?' Jacko asked Matt,
as soon as he could get him alone.

'She found me.' Matt feigned the blasé air of
a man of the world.

'Yeah, sure,' laughed Jacko. 'I tell you what
mate, you are the luckiest man in Summer
Bay. She is a little dolly.'

Matt wasn't sure about the 'dolly' part, but
he couldn't argue about being the luckiest
man in the Bay. As he accompanied Amanda
home through the dark, he felt like he was
walking on air. He could feel her hand inside

his own. His sense of unease had vanished. He knew that he would kiss her when they got back to the caravan, and he knew that she would respond. The unspoken messages that passed between them on the dance floor had told him this, had told him that his earlier nervousness had been unnecessary. She wanted to kiss him as much as he wanted to kiss her, and she would think none the less of him for initiating the moment.

Amanda slipped her key into the lock and opened the door of the caravan. She turned to Matt, her face half-lit by moonlight.

'Goodnight,' she murmured.

He took her chin in one hand and slowly lowered his lips to hers. His hesitation came not from lack of confidence, but from a desire to savour the moment. Both sensed that they were moving into adulthood with this one act. All previous kisses had been fumbling experiments. Now, for the first time, they were kissing somebody they really wanted to kiss.

Slowly Matt's lips met hers. He explored their soft pliancy, touching them gently with his tongue. Amanda closed her eyes. She felt that she was falling into a well, that she was tumbling head over heels into darkness. She surrendered herself to the delicious feeling, to the strong sensations of his arms around her, of his body pressed against her, of his mouth on hers. Suddenly her head started to spin and she pulled back, alarmed.

'What?' Matt was worried that he had misread the signals.

'I'm scared.'

'I didn't mean to . . .' Matt was mortified. He had gone too far.

Amanda hurried to reassure him.

'You didn't do anything wrong. It was wonderful. But a bit too wonderful. I've only just met you and things are . . . I don't know, they seem to be going too quickly. You see . . . if you'd gone on much longer, I'd have asked you in.'

She gestured back into the caravan.

'You know what that would have meant. I wouldn't have been able to help myself. And that scares me, because that's something I always told myself I'd only do if I really, really loved someone. You'd better go.'

She darted forward and pecked him gently on the cheek.

Matt felt deflated. Was she telling him that it

was all over before it had even begun? Was her fear of wanting to go too far going to make her finish it now?

'I want to see you tomorrow.' He had to say it.

'I want to see you too. I want to spend all day with you, if that's okay. I don't know if I can hang out till then to be honest.'

Matt beamed when he heard this. It wasn't the end after all.

'That's how I feel too. I'll be here at six. We'll catch some early morning waves.'

'You catch them, I'll watch,' Amanda laughed. 'You saw how terrible I was today.'

'You'll make a fantastic surfer one day,' he reassured her. 'It just takes time to get your balance.'

He kissed her again gently.

'Six o'clock. I know it sounds corny, but I'll dream about you.'

'It doesn't sound corny at all,' she said, as she returned the kiss.

Matt strode off into the night, feeling like a million bucks. How could life be so good?

When Amanda turned out the light and lay

down to sleep, she felt warm and secure. It didn't really matter to her any more what had happened eleven years ago in Summer Bay. All that mattered was what was happening now.

As she sank into a deep sleep, her father paced the First Class Lounge in Honolulu Airport. Mechanical failure had delayed his flight for eight hours; eight hours that could mean the difference between having his daughter's love and losing it. He'd tried to transfer flights, but was unable to do so. Everything seemed to be conspiring against him. Was it fate catching up with him at last? One thing was definite, he vowed to himself. If he didn't arrive too late, he would take Amanda as far away from Summer Bay as possible. And he'd make sure she never saw the place or its residents again.

Celia was hovering vulture-like as Alf and Roo drove into the caravan park. They had rung to say they'd be returning early.

'Wouldn't you know, Ruthy. She can't wait to get the latest scuttlebut on Morag.'

The Stewart sisters had conducted an on-going feud for years. Celia considered her elder sister to be an acid-tongued harpy, while Morag returned the compliment by accusing the youngest of the family of being a narrow-minded, desiccated spinster. There was a germ of truth in each opinion.

'I think they're funny,' smiled Ruth, 'The way they both go red and splutter when they talk about each other.'

'Yeah, well she'd better not start now. I'm not in the mood.'

Celia bustled over to the car as it drew to a halt.

'I must talk to you, Alfred. It's imperative.'

'It's a pain in the bum, that's what it is.' Alf Stewart was not a man to mince words.

'I wouldn't bother, Alfred, if it wasn't of the utmost importance.'

'If it's about Morag . . .'

'Oh,' humphed Celia. 'As if I'm interested in the doings of that wretched woman. No, this is another matter entirely.'

Alf grabbed their bags from the boot and led the way inside.'

'A moment alone, please Ruth,' Celia said, as she guided Roo from the back door, through the living room and into the hall-way. 'This is not a matter for young ears.'

Roo smiled to herself as she climbed the stairs to her bedroom. She heard her father's gruff warning.

'This had better be good Celia.'

Then her aunt continued in hushed tones. Roo stood on the stairs listening, curious. Probably it was nothing. Another feud between Aunty Celia and her gossip cronies, Betty and Doris. She could only catch snatches of what was said.

The girl's name is Amanda Burton . . . if she asks you . . . it's a matter best buried . . . such a shocking tragedy . . . her friend's family's happiness destroyed by fate.'

Roo was mystified when she heard the vehemence of her father's reply.

'Fate, my eye. I still say the mongrel killed her.'

'There was no evidence of that,' said Celia.

'Ruddy courts. How much do they need?' Alf had no great opinion of the country's judicial system. 'It was as plain as the nose on your face.'

'It's a matter for the Lord on judgement day now. No one escapes the great court in the sky.'

Celia preened, rather taken with her turn of phrase.

'I saw the little kiddy,' Alf replied gruffly. 'If that wasn't evidence, nothin' is; all battered and bruised. I tell you what, if I'd 'a' got my hands on the mongrel back then, he wouldn't have had to wait to get what was comin' to him.'

'Alfred, hush. Roo may hear.'

The mention of her name pricked Roo's conscience. She knew she shouldn't be listening. She hurried on up the stairs, noticing as she did so that Alf lowered his voice in response to Celia's warning.

'It must be something serious for dad to pay attention to Aunty Celia,' she thought. 'Otherwise he'd just tell her to shut up. I wonder what they're talking about?'

In the living room, the discussion was coming to a close. Alf was not a man to waste time worrying at a topic once he'd made up his mind.

'Okay, sis, you're right. It's none of the girl's business, whoever she is, so if she comes askin' questions I'll tell her I don't have a clue.'

'Bravo Alfred, bravo.'

'So, what's goin' on? Are you turnin' over a new leaf or somethin'?'

'What do you mean?'

'Well, it's not like you to pass up a chance to gossip. I'd 'a' thought you'd be maggin' to your cronies about it by now. Rakin' up the dirt.'

'I am not speaking to Betty Fallwell and Doris Peters at the moment. Besides, certain things are too unpleasant to be spoken of. Such a shocking death . . . to mull over it, especially after eleven years, would be ghoulish in the extreme.'

Unaware of this discussion, Amanda lay sunning herself contentedly on the beach. The morning had been one of the most wonderful experiences of her life. Matt had arrived promptly at six, as he had promised, and they had hurried down to the beach to watch the sunrise.

As they'd seated themselves on the sand, the first glow of dawn was making itself felt on the horizon. Matt had sat close to her, then had slipped his arm around her waist. She'd laid her head against his shoulder and felt his lips brush against her hair in response. She'd been filled with a feeling that was both peaceful and unsettling; peaceful in the absolute rightness of being there with him, unsettling in the emotions that it prompted. She had only just met this boy and yet she felt . . . what?

She felt in love. She couldn't deny it, even if she was confused by the fact. She'd read about love, seen movies about it, talked to her friends about it, but until now she could only imagine what it was like. Now she knew, and the sheer speed with which it had happened both elated and frightened her.

Before her, on the horizon, the sun had started to lift into view; first a fingernail sliver of brilliance, then a shimmering semicircle, then finally its entire radiance making the eyes squint in self-protection as the rays reflected off the sea.

'I'm in heaven,' she'd thought, and nestled closer to Matt. Matt had then lifted her face to his and kissed her slowly and deeply. He'd felt so sure in doing this. Overnight, he had moved through the stage of confusion about his feelings. He loved her. He knew it. It was a fact.

The sun was now high in the sky, as they both lay face down on their towels, basking in their new-found happiness.

'Roo might be home by now.' Matt broke the silence. 'You want to go up and check?'

'I don't know if I can be bothered.'

Matt propped himself up on his elbow and looked at her.

'How come?'

'None of it seems very important any more.'

'Aren't you still curious?'

'Sort of. Not really.' Amanda could say this with confidence. 'Sure, that's why I came here. But what does it really matter? Whatever happened back then doesn't change the fact I love Daddy and it doesn't change the fact I . . .'

She broke off and blushed. She had almost said 'I love you'. She would have felt totally stupid if she had. It was too soon for that, even if she felt it.

Matt knew what she'd been about to say. He was glad she hadn't too. There was plenty of time for that later. But it made him feel on top of the world that she felt as he did. He filled the silence to help cover her embarrassment.

'The less time you're off asking questions, the more time we can have together. So it's fine by me.'

'That's how I feel too.' She sighed contentedly and turned on her back. The sun immediately bit at her skin, so she applied protector from the bottle at her side. 'I'll always be glad I remembered those things, whatever they were about. If I hadn't, I'd never have come here and if I hadn't come here, I'd never have met you. And if I hadn't met you . . . I don't know . . . I'd have been miserable.'

'It wouldn't have made any difference to you,' laughed Matt. 'You can't miss something that doesn't happen.'

'I'd have known somehow.' Amanda smiled at him gently. 'I'd have sensed it should have happened and didn't. I mightn't have known *what* I was missing, but I would have known I was missing *something*.'

She leaned across and kissed him. Matt laughed.

'I hope you know what you just said, cos it was sorta double dutch to me.'

Amanda took a breath to rephrase it, then laughed too.

'I know what I meant and that's all that matters. I love you.'

They both started. There it was. It had snuck out, despite the very recent warning to be on guard against it. It was too late to take it back, so Amanda just shrugged and smiled.

'Crazy, huh?'

'Yeah, crazy,' said Matt, but his expression showed just how he felt. 'I . . . oh, what the hell. I love you too, even if I have only known you a bit more than a day.'

She lay back on the sand as he moved towards her, wrapping her in his arms. They kissed.

'I don't care what happens,' Matt sighed. 'I don't care that you live in the city and I live here, or that you're rich and I'm poor, or that we're only fourteen, or . . . any practical stuff. I'm not going to stop seeing you. I couldn't.'

'Me neither.' Amanda reached her mouth up to his again. She knew that there were barriers against this becoming more than a holiday romance, but right now she didn't care about them either. They could be dealt with when the time came.

Floss and Neville made a funny-looking pair, as they waddled along the road into town.

'Looks like love is in the air, Floss old girl. That's young Matt and Amanda, isn't it?'

Floss's blood froze, as she looked down and saw the happy couple on the beach below.

'The sooner she gets out of town the better,' she muttered. Neville was puzzled.

'Don't tell me you're turnin' into a prude, Flossie?'

'It's got nothing to do with that. If they want a bit of a kiss and a cuddle, good luck to them. I'm just worried about what I saw in the cards. If young Amanda's out of town then no harm can come to her.'

'Don't you think that you're takin' it just a bit too seriously?' Nev knew his wife was good. But being able to see someone's death? That was trusting the cards a bit too much.

'All I know is, better safe than sorry.'

Floss lowered her head and bustled on. She still felt guilty about going behind Amanda's back, so guilty that she'd not even told Nev about it. She just couldn't understand where Amanda's father was. He should have had plenty of time to get here by now. Maybe the housekeeper hadn't passed on the message.

'God, I hope she did.'

'What was that, old girl?'

Floss realized that her anxiety had made her speak her thoughts.

'Nothin' Nev, nothin'. Maybe I'm losin' my marbles.'

A car approached.

'Gawd look at that,' said Nev. 'A Rolls. Someone's got money.'

Floss's heart soared. It had to be him. She could tell from going through Amanda's things that they were wealthy. She felt sure that this was Mr Taylor on his way to the caravan park.

'You go on ahead, Nev,' she said. 'There's somethin' I've got to do.'

Neville looked at her, totally bemused, as she flagged down the luxury car.

'Go on. I'll catch up with you.'

'Maybe she is losin' her marbles,' thought Neville, as he trudged towards town, looking back over his shoulder to see the driver wind down his window to Floss.

'Mr Taylor?' asked Floss.

'Yes.' Bernard was bemused. How could this woman possibly know?

'I'm the one who called.' Floss wasted no time in getting to the heart of the matter. 'If you love your daughter you'll get her away from here as soon as you can. She's down on the beach there. Take her away, get her out of town. Now. It's important.'

The bizarre old woman hurried away, before

Bernard could even thank her for her intervention or question her about her strange warning. As he alighted from the car to call her back, he glanced down to the beach. He froze. There, with some boy, was Amanda. His eyes narrowed and his temper rose, as he registered the passionate embrace.

'Amanda!'

Amanda recoiled out of Matt's arms, as she heard her father's voice. She stared in disbelief, as she saw him coming across the sand towards her.

'Daddy?'

'Get in the car, Amanda . . .'

'But Daddy . . .'

'I said get in the car.'

Matt got up. He wasn't sure what was going on, but he didn't want Amanda's father getting the wrong idea.

'Mr Taylor, I think . . .'

'I don't know who you are boy and I don't care. Just keep away from my daughter.'

Amanda was horrified.

'Daddy, we weren't . . .'

'You lied to me, Amanda. You went behind my back, you ran away to come here and I discover you letting a virtual stranger maul you in public. It makes me wonder if I really know you at all.'

'Daddy, I . . .'

'Get up to the car,' Bernard roared, grabbing her by the arm and almost throwing her in the direction of the roadway.

Matt was at a complete loss. What could he do? He watched Amanda being dragged across the sand towards the car.

'He's her father after all. He does have the right.'

Then his temper flared. He and Amanda had rights too. He ran and caught up with them just as Bernard Taylor threw his daughter into the car.

'You can't do this, Mr Taylor. Amanda and I love each other.'

All Matt got for his pain was a forceful hand in the chest, that sent him sprawling to the ground. Before he could overcome his shock and regain his feet, Bernard Taylor had leapt into the car, started it and driven away in a cloud of dust.

The last Matt saw of Amanda was her face

staring back at him through the rear window. Then the car turned the bend and she was gone.

chapter six

Amanda stared disconsolately out of the window of the hired limousine, as she was driven north from Geneva to Neuchatel. Her father sat beside her, a barrier of stoney silence between them. The spectacular mountain scenery of the Jura made little impression on them, locked as they both were in thought.

The last week had been full of bitter arguments and recriminations. Their formerly love-filled relationship had deteriorated into one of mutual suspicion and hostility. Amanda simply couldn't understand her father's reaction; his rage, his demands that she should never return to Summer Bay, his fierce rejection of any questions about the past. Initially she had tried to reason with him, to assure him that her relationship with Matt was something wonderful and gentle, not a smutty summer dalliance. But soon she realized that his aversion was towards the sleepy seaside town, not the boy she now loved.

'I won't ask any questions, if that's what you want. I'll never go there again. He can come and see me. Just let me see him, that's all. I love him.'

'You're too young to know the meaning of the word.'

His instant rejection of her feelings infuriated her. She was not a child.

'If I'm old enough to know my father's a liar who's scared of what I'll find in Summer Bay, I'm old enough to know who I love.'

She regretted the words as soon as she'd said them.

Anger fuelled his reply.

'I've made enquiries about a school in Switzerland. I'll confirm the booking. We'll leave the day after tomorrow.'

She couldn't believe it. He was exiling her to some Swiss academy for the daughters of the rich, rather than risk her returning to Summer Bay.

'You can't stop me from going back for ever,' she flared. Now her suspicions were out in the open she may as well let him have it. 'What happened in Summer Bay that's so terrible? Telling me can't be any worse than sending me away.'

'I'm simply removing you from temptation. It's for your own good.'

'Why? At least tell me why. I know it's not Matt.'

'Perhaps one day. When you're old enough to understand. Now . . .'

'You're just hoping I'll forget about it. Well I won't. Never! You can send me overseas for as long as you like. The first thing I'll do when I'm free is come back and go to Summer Bay and ask all the questions I like. You might just as well tell me now.'

Her defiance fell on deaf ears. The decision was made.

Later that afternoon she tried to use the phone to call Matt. She found that locks had been installed. It couldn't be used without a key. She left the house, determined to walk down the road to the pay-phone. Suddenly her father was there, guiding her forcefully back inside. That night she climbed out of her bedroom window and tried to run away. But the alarm devices installed to keep burglars out were just as effective for keeping someone in. She set off one of the sensitive devices and was discovered hurrying out of the front gate.

It sickened her to realize that she was a prisoner in the home that had previously represented all that was warm and loving in her life.

The next day her father suddenly took her up to her room and locked the door. She thought she heard Matt's voice raised in anger. She thought she heard him calling that he loved her, but that was all she could make out. She called and banged on her bedroom door, but to no avail. If Matt heard her, he was clearly in no position to do anything about it. He'd no doubt been whisked from the property and deposited unceremoniously on the pavement. Her bedroom faced the rear of the grounds, so she could only guess.

That night at dinner, she questioned her father. He admitted that it was Matt she'd heard, but that the boy's rough and loutish behaviour had simply reinforced Bernard's view that sending her away was the right thing to do.

'Nothing Matt did could be worse than what you're doing. I thought I loved you, but I don't. I hate you.'

It was as if she had lashed him with a whip. He flinched, then he controlled himself.

'You'll thank me one day.'

So here she was, being driven into the picture postcard beauty of the Swiss mountains, heading for the College des Bergs, the school that would become home for the next three years.

If she could only have seen the turmoil in her father's mind, she would have perhaps been less harsh on him. Bernard Taylor was confused and scared. He was desperately and illogically grasping at straws, hoping that the greatest secret of his life could be kept hidden. He was unsure of the ultimate outcome of his actions, but he felt that he had no alternative.

There was no doubt that Amanda would resent, probably even hate him. But time heals. At best, she would settle into her new environment and forget her questions and this childish infatuation that fuelled them. At worst, they would remain with her, but she would be in no position to discover the truth until she was old enough to deal with it maturely.

Her mail would be vetted; correspondence to or from Summer Bay would be suppressed. Not that it was likely any letters would arrive from there. It was impossible for Matt to discover Amanda's new address, unless her friends wrote to him on her behalf. And as all mail from the school was censored, any such move could be forestalled. Bernard had explained the situation to the headmistress in terms designed to elicit her cooperation. Amanda was unreasonably infatuated and had to be saved from the attentions of this lower-class opportunist. 'Better to lose her love for a few years than lose it for ever,' he thought, as the car drove into the grounds of the College des Bergs.

As father and daughter alighted, the headmistress emerged and came down the front steps of the impressive building. Bernard took in the surroundings with satisfaction. A beautiful converted chateau set amidst snow-capped peaks, where Amanda would meet the daughters of some of the wealthiest men in the world. Slowly it would work its magic and make her forget the little seaside resort and the bin man's son who lived there.

'Bonjour. Bienvenue au collège. Welcome. I am Madame Lantier, your headmistress.'

The attractive fifty-year-old woman smiled broadly and benevolently.

'She looks like a vampire,' thought Amanda. She was not prepared to give Madame Lantier the benefit of the doubt.

Her farewells with her father were brief and cold. As Bernard drove back down the mountain, he had another crisis of confidence. He hoped to God that he was doing the right thing.

That night Amanda dreamt that she was back in the caravan in Summer Bay. Her father was beating her to death, pounding her with his fists, making her ribs crack as he smashed down on her chest.

She woke up crying, lathered in sweat.

The image she brought out of the dream was of herself standing in the doorway of the caravan watching her father as he murdered her.

A question played through her brain, as she sunk back into sleep. 'How can you be in two places at once? How could I watch myself being murdered?' And somehow she knew that in the answer to that lay the answer to the entire mystery.

The next morning when she awoke she knew that she had dreamed, but try as she might, she could recall nothing of her nightmare. She showered, dressed and grimly faced her first day in prison. For the first time in her life she understood the meaning of the phrase to which she could never previously relate:

Poor little rich girl.

A visit to Amanda's caravan, after the Rolls Royce had swept out of sight, proved fruitless. Matt found all of her belongings gone. The evacuation had been so swift that not even Alf was aware of it. It was Matt who found the note and the money pinned to the caravan door.

FOR THREE DAYS ACCOMMODATION $60.00 THANKYOU.

Matt could imagine the scene; Amanda tearfully being forced to gather together her belongings while her father hastily scribbled a few words and counted out the three twenty dollar bills. No doubt he hurried her along, concerned that Matt would arrive and cause a scene, perhaps even get from Amanda what he so desperately wanted: her address.

Matt took the note and the money to Alf and explained the situation. Alf, and Celia who was also there, reacted mysteriously.

As Matt explained that Amanda had booked in under a false name, that her name was actually Amanda Taylor, Celia muttered: 'Well that explains it all.'

Alf looked grim and added:

'It's a good thing I didn't see the mongrel. I'd have given him what he's had coming for years.'

'What do you mean?' Matt asked. This sounded hopeful. 'Do you know something about Amanda's dad? That's what she was down here for, you know; trying to find things out.'

Alf suddenly looked shifty and denied any particular knowledge, trying to cover what he'd said.

'All I meant was I wish I'd been there to stop the bloke roughing up his daughter. I wish I could 'a' stuck up for yous.'

Matt knew he was lying, but for the life of him he couldn't understand why. This situation was becoming more mysterious by the minute.

When he left them, he ran across Roo coming back from the shops. Maybe he could get some joy here.

'Just the person I want to see.'

'Yeah?' smiled Roo. 'What have I done?'

'Nothing,' he replied. 'I know this sounds crazy, but try to remember; way back; to when you were three. Can you remember a girl called Amanda Taylor coming to the caravan park? We played with her, you and me. Does that ring any sort of bell?'

Roo considered, then shrugged.

'No, why?'

'It doesn't matter. It was just a long shot.'

'You say it was the three of us? You played with her too?'

'Yeah.'

'Can you remember anything?'

Matt shook his head. 'That's why I asked. One other thing. Have your Dad and Celia been acting strange today?'

'No. Well sort of.'

'What do you mean?'

'Aunty Celia was flapping on about some girl.' The coincidence suddenly hit Roo. 'It's funny, her name was Amanda too. Amanda Burton though.'

'What did they say?' Matt's eyes lit up.

'I only caught bits of it. Something about a kid being killed, a family tragedy or . . . I don't know. Anyway, it sounded like someone hurt a kid and got away with it. Dad was really angry. He seemed to think the guy should have been charged. Something like that. Like I said, I could only hear bits.'

'That's enough. Thanks.'

Matt hurried off, realizing immediately what he had to do. He knew Alf well enough to know that asking him more questions was useless. Once this bluff ocker decided a subject was out of bounds there was no budging him.

'Anyway,' Matt thought 'I don't need him. Or Celia.'

Now that he knew the secret was connected with something as newsworthy as the death of a child, he realized there was a much better source of information.

He hurried into the offices of the *Summer Bay Courier* and played the eager student.

'Hi Mr Dawson.'

Graham Dawson was the editor.

'I'm doing a project for school on the development of Summer Bay.' Matt's blue-eyed innocence was highly plausible. 'I have to choose one particular summer and compare it with how things are now. I'm going to go back eleven years. Should be long enough to make a bit of difference. Could I look at your old papers from the summer of eleven years ago?'

Dawson was more than eager to please, but he had to get the appropriate microfilm out of storage. It would be ready for Matt in the morning.

Matt returned home, trying to will time to pass quickly. He refused any dinner and locked himself away in his bedroom.

It was eight o'clock when his mother knocked and told him that Floss was there to see him.

'Could you tell her to go away please?'

This was the last thing he needed.

'She seems pretty upset about something.'

'She'll just want to say she's sorry about me and Amanda. Say thanks and that I'm not feeling well. It's sort o' true anyway.'

Suddenly Floss appeared in the doorway behind Dawn.

'I don't mean to take too much on myself, Dawn.' She indicated back towards the living room where she'd been told to wait. 'I just have to see Matt though, and I guessed he'd want me sent packing. Please, lovey?'

The last words were directed to Matt. A plea.

He considered for a few moments and then nodded, indicating for her to come in. He

115

could feel her agitation and sensed there
was a lot more than sympathy behind the
call. Dawn retired discreetly. It was none of
her affair.

'If you love Amanda, sweety,' Floss began,
as she perched on the end of the bed,
'You'll forget about her. Trust me, it's for
the best.'

'How do you know what's best for us?' Matt
couldn't keep the annoyance from his voice.
What business was it of hers anyway?

'Laugh if you want to, but I've seen it in the
cards.' She hurried on before Matt could
interrupt. 'I can't quite explain it, it's a mystery to me even though I've seen it, but I
know it's so. How can I put it?'

She hesitated a few moments, collected her
thoughts and then continued.

'Unless we do whatever we can to change
the message in the cards, Amanda will die
here in Summer Bay. And you'll be with
her.'

Matt started to protest.

'Hear me out.' Floss's total conviction made
her forceful. 'That's why I was so frightened
every time I saw you two together. I was
fearful for the girl's safety. That's the future.

There's another part to what I saw though. The past. That's the bit I can't understand. Amanda's already died before, you see. I know that sounds crazy, but that's what I saw in the cards. She's died once in Summer Bay already and she'll die here again; unless we change things.'

'A person can't die twice, Floss.' Matt shook his head. The poor old thing was going potty.

'You don't have to tell me it sounds weird. But I know what I saw, even if I don't know what it means. I tell you somethin', and you listen. You go searchin' her out and bringin' her back here, and you'll be killin' her as surely as if you'd taken a gun and shot her. Let her go, lovey. If you love her, you'll forget you ever met her.'

She stood, smoothed her dress and moved to the door.

'That's all there is to say. No point in gnawing at it like an old bone. It's up to you now.'

And she was gone.

Matt was totally dismissive of what Floss said. He'd seen a programme on TV about a disease that hit old people, made them go funny in the head. Senile Dementia it was

117

called. Matt really liked old Floss and Nev. He hoped for their sakes that it was nothing like this. Sure he'd taken Amanda to Floss himself, knowing that she told people some pretty accurate things. But this was a totally different ballgame. Amanda dying twice? It was nuts.

The next morning, however, as he scrolled through the microfilm at the Courier office, his jaw hit the ground. It couldn't be. But there it was in black and white in front of him. He suddenly realized that Floss's powers were indeed astonishing. She was no senile old woman, she was a gifted clairvoyant. The paper was dated December 22nd, 1978. And the lead article gave the entire puzzling affair a startling clarity.

Matt's heart sank as he walked from the newspaper office to Floss and Neville's van. The initial thrill of discovery was dulled as he remembered what Floss had said.

'Let her go, lovey. If you love her, you'll forget you even met her.'

It was hard for him to credit Floss with the power to foresee Amanda dead. But if she'd had the power to see into the past, even if she hadn't realized the meaning of her cryptic vision, surely she could be just as right about the future. And if she was, it was dangerous for Amanda to be around him.

He still found it hard to believe the whole thing, but he couldn't deny the evidence of his own eyes. He knew what he'd read in the paper.

Matt was still wrestling with his dilemma as he walked across the caravan park and knocked at the door of the wagon.

Floss was relieved to have her vision confirmed by hard evidence.

'That's the terrible thing about having the power, you see, lovey. You know you're right, but if you can't prove it . . . it makes you feel like you're going mad.'

'I bet.' Matt could understand. He remembered his suspicions about her sanity the night before.

'Nev and I weren't in Summer Bay back then,' she continued, 'So of course we knew nothin' about all that. I'd have put two and two together straight off if we had. So that's it. That's how someone can die twice. Yeah, it makes sense when you think about it. There's no doubt about the power of the cards . . .'

'I have to go and see her Floss.'

Floss started, as he cut across her ramblings.

'Now lovey, don't you realize . . .'

'Just one last time. If only I knew where she was. I want to see her one last time so I can say goodbye properly. I've never loved anyone before, see. I feel like someone's dug a hole in the pit of my stomach. I have to let her know I'll never forget her, that's all. I'm not going to risk her life. I wouldn't.'

Floss looked at him thoughtfully.

'I know where she is, lovey.'

'You do?' Matt was thrown. How could she?

'I'm not proud to admit it, but I did some snooping. There are other things I did I'm not too proud of either, but I'd rather not go into those. I did 'em for the good of the lass though. You absolutely promise me you're going there to say your goodbyes and to make sure she never comes back to Summer Bay, and I'll tell you where she is.'

'I promise.'

Floss looked deep into his eyes. Having satisfied herself that he was being honest with himself as well as her, she took a piece of paper and wrote on it.

'You're a fine kid, lovey. You're both fine

kids. I'm just sorry it had to work out this way.'

Matt caught the first bus out of town.

52 Gramercy Crescent, Vaucluse, was an impressive mansion set back from the road on a lavish two acres of grounds. Matt hesitated at the gates, feeling somewhat intimidated by the surroundings. But he steeled himself, strode up the drive and rang the bell.

Bernard Taylor's face was grim as he opened the door.

'I suggest you leave immediately young man, before I call the police.'

'I have to see Amanda, sir. It's very important.'

'I'm sure it is.' There was an unpleasant edge to Bernard's voice. 'I noticed you arrive. I've made sure Amanda is out of the way. You will not be seeing her now or, if I have my way, ever.'

'I don't want to, sir. Except this once more. That's why I'm here. I just wanted to say goodbye properly and explain things to her. If you'll just let me explain why I can't see her again.'

'You can't see her again because I say so.'

It was hard for Matt to remain civil with this man, now that he knew the lies he'd cowered behind over the years. But he had to keep his cool. If he argued with Bernard Taylor, he'd have no chance of seeing Amanda.

'I can imagine what you'll explain,' Bernard continued. 'No doubt you've discovered the answers to Amanda's questions and you've come here to share them with her.'

'No sir, I . . .'

'Tell me you don't know what happened. Look me in the eye and tell me.'

Surprised by this demand, Matt was betrayed by his basic honesty.

'I thought so,' snapped Bernard.

'I know what happened sir, but . . .'

Bernard was in no mood to listen.

'I suggest you leave now before my security service arrives. I've already called them. They're no doubt on their way.'

'I'm not going to tell Amanda about that, believe me. I just want to say goodbye and tell her I love her. I don't want her thinking that I just forgot about her. You've got to trust me.'

'Do you really think I'm going to risk the integrity of the son of a garbage man?'

Matt was shocked to discover that Bernard knew about his background. Surely Amanda wouldn't have told him. Surely she wouldn't have described him in that way. Or would she? His insecurity made him smart.

Bernard was shrewd enough to register the reaction and to capitalize on it.

'Oh yes, that's how Amanda summed you up. The bin man's son. You don't really think you were anything more than a casual diversion for her?'

'I know I was.' Matt could feel his colour rising. He could hear all the old childhood taunts, the voices he had stilled by his expertise on a surfboard. But surfing skills meant nothing to this vicious, unpleasant man, living as he did in his harbourside mansion. To him, the son of a bin man was not much better than the rubbish his father collected.

'You think you're so special, don't you?' he yelled at Bernard.

The rush of insecurity made him lose control. He couldn't think clearly. If he had, he'd have realized a man like Bernard Taylor had obtained a full rundown on him from his security service. It was ordered the previous night and delivered that morning.

'My old man might have a cruddy job,' he continued angrily, 'But at least he's a good father. What are you? A liar and a murderer.'

Bernard blanched.

'Get out of here, before I throw you out,' he roared.

'Yeah, you can't hack the truth, can you? Better a bloke should shovel garbage than kill his kid.'

As the security patrol drove into the grounds, they saw a young man flailing out at Bernard Taylor and yelling at the top of his voice. They did not stop to question whether he was defending himself from the furious Bernard's blows or attacking the man who had called them. Naturally, in their minds, it was the latter.

'He's a liar and a murderer, Amanda!!' Matt yelled, hoping that she would hear him. 'Your old man's a liar and a murderer!!! Don't believe a word he says. I love you, Amanda. Whatever he tells you, I love you.'

He was dragged, kicking and screaming, into the security patrol's car and was driven straight to the police station. Bernard agreed not to press charges on the condition that he return immediately to Summer Bay. A restraining order was taken out against him, forbidding him to go anywhere near the Taylor mansion.

Gary Wilson came down and picked his son up from the police station, totally mystified about what had got into him. Matt told him nothing. What was the point?

As they drove into Summer Bay, they passed the local rubbish dump. Matt stared at it bitterly. It had been the bane of his childhood. He thought he'd beaten his old insecurities; but, with a little prompting from Bernard Taylor, they'd returned with the same force and bitterness he'd felt on the day he'd got back at Lance and Martin. This time it was different though. Then he was just a kid, getting his own back on kids. Now he was fighting in the adult world, where the rich had power and the poor had none. This was reality. No amount of skill on his surfboard was going to resolve this situation. He had lost the girl he loved and he would never be able to tell her why. There was no justice.

chapter seven

Hubble, bubble, toil and trouble.

Celia and her two cronies, Betty and Doris, sat outside Ailsa's store like the three witches from 'Macbeth', mixing a potent brew of gossip.

'Poor, dear Matthew,' said Celia. 'Who can blame him for going to rack and ruin?'

'Hmm.' Doris wasn't convinced. 'It doesn't excuse his terrible rudeness yesterday. I was visiting Dawn when he came home and he no more than grunted at me. He's driving his poor mother to despair, you know.'

'And his father, my dear.' Betty, the minor league gossip of the three, was thrilled to have some direct information to add. She'd had a long talk with Matt's mother just that morning. 'He won't even speak to poor Gary, Dawn says. She can't make the boy out. He's bottling it all up inside, that's the problem. She says that if he could only get his feelings out in the open he'd be all right. And a mother should know, shouldn't she?'

'It's two months for heaven's sakes.' Doris had no time for such emotional self-indulgence. 'And he's only fourteen. It's not like it was true love. Children of that age don't know what love is.'

'Romeo and Juliet were fourteen, Doris. Let us not underestimate the emotions of youth.' Celia, a victim of blighted romance herself, was always on the side of the heart-broken.

'Yes. Look what happened to poor Romeo and Juliet, Doris.' Betty was wide-eyed at the prospect of teenage tragedy in their midst. 'Dawn and Gary had better keep a very close watch on Matt.'

'Oh pish tush,' Celia chastised her friend. 'Matthew is made of much sterner stuff than that, despite his current behaviour. Some of us . . .'

Celia bowed her head solemnly to indicate that she was speaking of herself and the death of her beloved fiancé, Les, in Vietnam. '. . . some of us have truly suffered, Betty and have come through the refining fire of tragedy. We can understand what young Matthew is experiencing, albeit on a much smaller scale than what we went through when our own love was so cruelly blighted.'

Celia always lapsed into the use of the royal

127

'we' when talking about the pain in her past.

'There he is now.'

Celia, in full flight, was peeved by the sharp dig in the ribs which accompanied Betty's warning.

The loquacious trio watched Matt approach; Doris disapproving, Betty boggle-eyed and Celia empathetic.

'I shall speak to him.' Celia made a spur of the moment decision. 'If anyone can reach him it is I; I who have suffered in a like, nay, greater, way.'

The three gossips were not exaggerating about one thing. The last two months had been a time of great blackness and cynicism for Matt. He had spiralled in upon himself, turning his back on his family, his surfing, his schoolwork and his friends. He had become a brooding loner, eaten away by a yearning for Amanda and disillusionment in the world. He lived in his thoughts now, hitting out at anyone who tried to get through to him.

'Matthew!!! A moment please.'

Matt felt his bile rise at the sound of Celia's voice. He could see her two cronies watching eagerly in the background as she hurried towards him.

'Get lost!' he wanted to scream, but his conditioning made him modify it to:

'Not now, Miss Stewart.'

'But Matthew . . .'

'I said, not now.'

His tone was harsh, final. He turned on his heel and walked directly away from her, in a path that now took him down towards the beach.

'But Matthew . . .'

He wheeled on her, forcing himself not to shout.

'I know what you're going to say, Miss Stewart and, excuse me, but it's none of your business.' He called past Celia to the other two old biddies. 'And it's none of yours either. Stop coming around and stirring up Mum. Keep out of it, okay!!'

'Well!!!' Celia returned to the table, steam coming from her ears. 'Heartache or no heartache, there is no excuse for such rudeness. I do believe you're right Doris. The boy has had long enough to get over it by now. And as you say, he is only fourteen.'

'What about Romeo and Juliet, Celia?' Doris was not one to suppress an 'I told you so'.

'I have said I was wrong, have I not Doris? There is no need for that.' Celia pondered for a moment. 'I think it is time I spoke to Dawn Wilson and suggested she take stern measures with Matthew. The time for namby-pambying is past.'

She strode off, Betty and Doris hurrying along in her wake. Celia was a much more interesting companion in this crusading mode than when she was championing the cause of star-crossed lovers. This they had to see.

Having changed direction to get away from Celia, Matt found himself walking along the beach. He tended to avoid it these days, knowing that he'd run into Jacko and the gang. He knew they meant well, but they always tried to urge him back into surfing. They couldn't understand his sudden rejection of the sport. He could hardly blame them for that though, when he couldn't find the words to explain it to them.

What he felt was too private to share. He couldn't tell them that every time he looked at his board he thought of Amanda, could see her laughing as she tried to stand, could see her tumbling off it and into his arms, could see her slapping the water in mock-frustration at her inability to balance. So much of their few days together had been spent in the water, playing around like this. Bad enough the constant emptiness in the pit of his stomach, without adding the extra pain that came with these once happy images. So the board was banished to the roof of the garage. Out of sight, out of mind.

His eyes scanned the water. Flat as a mill pond. Good. That meant no Jacko and co. He could safely sit on the sand for a while without risking their well-intentioned urgings. But a pep talk was approaching from another and far less-likely source.

'Check it out, Marty,' said Lance, as the two wallies wandered on to the beach.

'Chicks?' Martin looked up from the copy of *Playboy* that he'd just bought in Yabbie Creek. He didn't buy it from Ailsa's in case his Mum found out.

'No; Matt.'

'What's the big deal about that, dork-brain?'

'Nothin', I just feel sorry for him, that's all.'

'You what?' Martin didn't understand his mate sometimes.

'I feel sorry for him,' Lance repeated, thinking Martin hadn't heard.

'I caught what you said, mate, I just didn't believe you said it. Mattie-Poohs got what he had comin'. He wouldn't 'a' been kicked in the guts if he hadn't stole that Amanda chick from me in the first place. Don't expect me to feel sorry for him.'

Martin was nothing if not a long-term grudge-bearer.

'Yeah, well I reckon it's a bummer, eh. Poor bloke looks miserable every time you see him.'

Lance was a kind-hearted fellow beneath all the bravado.

'This is the bloke who dumped cow poop on our heads.'

'That was yonks ago.'

'He still did it. You wanna play Mr Nice Guy, you can do it on your own, mate.'

Martin flopped on to the sand, and buried himself in the copious charms of Miss February.

'I've got better things to do. You need your head read.'

This was added at his mate's back, as Lance shuffled across towards Matt.

'Gidday.' Lance squatted down next to him.

'What do you want?' Matt asked, although his tone clearly indicated he wished Lance would forget the answer and just disappear.

'I'm not gonna bother you much, mate. Reckon you've got lots to think about, even if it is a while since everythin' happened. I just wanted to let you know I'm sorry, eh. Reckon I can understand. You see . . . 'n' don't tell Marty about this, cos he don't know nuthin' about it . . . I got kicked in the guts by a chick's old man once too. Micki Grubbs's old man. Course it was a long time ago . . . in kindy actually . . . but I can still remember it. He didn't want me doin' sandpit with her, cos he reckoned I was a nohoper. Reckoned I was always tryin' to kiss her. Well I was, but we were only little, eh? Reckon he had a real dirty mind to get steamed up over that.'

Lance paused for breath, then forged on.

'So, anyway, I know what it's like see. So if people tell you you're a dork for still feelin' bad after only two months, tell 'em to get nicked. Cos I still feel bad after twelve years. Catch you later.'

Emotion embarrassed Lance. Having had his say, he hurried away to avoid any gratitude.

Matt sat utterly still for a few moments, then a silent tear slid down his cheek. The bitterness and pain that he had stored up for months, that his mother had urged him to release, that he desperately tried to bring to the surface, had refused to come. All of the talks by his family, his friends, the deputy-head, Donald Fisher, who was concerned about his falling grades; all these things had failed to do what the good-hearted bozo had done. Lance had touched a chord.

'Hey look, Marty.' Lance nudged Martin away from Miss January. 'He's cryin'.'

Martin watched Matt's jerking, sobbing back.

'Bull, mate, he's laughin'. Whatever you said must 'a' been real funny. Good on you, mate, you cheered him up.'

That didn't seem right to Lance somehow. His story had not been a funny one. It had been meant as a sad acknowledgement to Matt that others had lived the same pain.

'Maybe he's laughin' at me,' Lance thought. 'Laughin' at me story.'

He felt betrayed, for he had dredged this experience up from his past at some emotional cost.

'Serves me right,' he thought, 'Tryin' to help. Marty's right. I shouldn't 'a' bothered.'

He would have felt differently if he could have seen Matt's face, contorted with the unhappiness of lost love. Lance, in his simple-minded way, had been exactly what Matt needed; he had been the key that opened the floodgates.

Bernard was in London when the news came of Amanda's collapse. He caught the first flight to Geneva and was in Neuchatel six hours later.

'The doctor is conducting tests,' Madame Lantier told him, as they walked down the corridor to the school's sick bay. 'I'm sure it's nothing to worry about. Amanda is simply . . . traumatisée . . . how do you say?'

'Over-wrought.'

'Exactly, Monsieur Taylor. She does not eat, she does not sleep. Time is not making her forget this young man.'

'She will forget,' snapped Bernard.

He was worried about his daughter, but he was also angry. Two months should have been long enough. Amanda should have started to forget by now, both about Matt and her obsessive desire for answers.

He was shocked out of his anger when he entered the sterile four-bed room. Amanda, the only occupant, lay pale against a mountain of pillows. She seemed frighteningly fragile and small.

'My poor baby.' Bernard hurried over to her. 'I came as soon as I heard.'

Tears welled in Amanda's eyes. Despite their last harsh meeting, this man was her father and she was feeling sick, scared and vulnerable.

'I feel terrible, Daddy.'

'You'll be fine sweetheart. You just have to start eating and sleeping properly.'

'It's more than that. I know it is.'

Amanda had started feeling weak about a month after her arrival in Neuchatel. At first, she had assumed it was just a symptom of her distress, of her longing for Matt. But as the days went by, her energy had dwindled until she felt like she was dragging herself through the day. She had not wanted to alarm anyone, in fact she was scared to mention the matter. She suspected that there was something seriously wrong with her and she wanted to bury her head in the sand. Perhaps it would just go away. That morning, however, she had felt as if she were living a dream; as if everyone and everything existed at a great distance from her. Then the blackness came and over-whelmed her. She awoke in the infirmary, with the doctor from the local hospital taking a blood sample and insisting that she be kept in bed until the results of the tests were known.

'There's nothing wrong with you that a good rest won't cure,' Bernard assured her. He put his arm around her and kissed her brow. 'I know none of this has been easy for you. I certainly know it's been terrible for me. But we won't talk about that tonight. I'm here with you my darling and we're not going to argue. We're just going to make sure you get better, aren't we?'

Part of Amanda wanted to hate this man, wanted to draw away from his embrace. But the other part, the scared little girl who sensed that there was something seriously wrong, needed his comfort. She snuggled into the crook of his arm and fell into a deep sleep.

She dreamed of Matt, as she had done every night for the last two months. In this dream she was riding down a wave beside him, the wind whistling through their hair. She was surfing as no woman had ever surfed before and Matt was calling encouragement across to her.

She woke briefly at three in the morning and felt Bernard's arm still around her. But she was only half-awake. She mistook the embrace for someone else's. She murmured contentedly and fell back into a deep slumber.

'Matt.'

Bernard tensed at the name that he had come to hate, the name that had come to symbolize his separation from his daughter. He smoothed the damp hair from her heated brow and suppressed the guilt that came flooding in behind his anger.

The next morning, Bernard's world fell apart. The doctor's face was grim as he broke the news.

'I'm sorry, Mr Taylor.'

'There must be some mistake. There has to be.'

'There is no mistake. I wish I could give you that hope. At the most, Amanda has a month to live. I can only offer you my sincerest condolences.'

'But . . .' Bernard couldn't focus his

thoughts. 'There has to be something you can do. Anything. I don't care how much it costs.'

'There is nothing. If you wish to obtain a second opinion . . .'

'Too bloody right I'm going to get a second opinion.'

He flew Amanda to London that afternoon. By the time they reached Heathrow she was exhausted. She collapsed at the airport and was rushed to hospital. Further tests simply confirmed the initial diagnosis.

'I think that Amanda should be told, Mr Taylor. She knows something serious is happening. I consider it wrong to keep the truth from the patient in cases such as this.'

'I'll tell her,' Bernard said. He knew the doctor was right, although it broke his heart to consider the prospect. 'It's my place to do it.'

Amanda knew what he was going to say as soon as he entered the room.

'I'm dying, aren't I?' It was a statement, not a question.

'Yes, darling.' Bernard had held back the tears for days. He could hold them back no longer.

'It's all right, it's all right.' Amanda was dry-eyed as she stroked her father's hand.

'I think I've known all along, somehow. Please don't cry, Daddy. It's not your fault.'

'Maybe if I'd . . .'

'It's got nothing to do with what's happened.' She squeezed his hand hard, making him look at her. She reached up and wiped away his tears. 'You musn't ever blame yourself. I love you, Daddy. I hated fighting. Let's not fight any more. I don't want to die here. Let me go home to die. You know where I want to be.'

Bernard Taylor sat shell-shocked as he realized what she was saying.

'I know you don't believe me, Daddy. I know you think it's just silly infatuation. But Matt's the only person I'll ever love now; in that way. And I do love him, Daddy. I have to see him before I die.'

Tears slid down her cheek, more for the pain she could see on her father's face than for her own suffering.

'I don't care any more about what happened all those years ago, unless you want to tell me. None of it seems at all important now. All that's important is to go home.'

Bernard sat very still. Then he nodded.

He had no choice.

The long plane journey back to Australia was agony for Amanda. It took its toll, despite all efforts to keep her comfortable. A twenty-four hour flight is draining enough for a healthy person, let alone one with only a few weeks to live.

As the plane flew the last leg from Singapore to Sydney, Amanda moaned in her sleep. Bernard, in the seat next to where she lay, grappled with his conscience. He owed her the truth, yet he feared it; he feared losing her so close to the end of her life. Should he remain a coward and accept her offer to bury the past? It would be so easy to. But no. He'd never be able to live with himself if he let her die without knowing.

'Amanda. Amanda darling, are you awake?' He must do it now, before his courage failed him.

Amanda stirred from her sleep and smiled gently. The pain had eased briefly. These were moments to be savoured.

'I'm going to tell you the truth. I promise you faithfully that it is the truth. Perhaps you'll hate me afterwards, perhaps you won't. Hopefully you'll be able to understand why I did what I felt I had to.'

'Are you sure?' Amanda had meant what she said when she'd offered to turn her back on it all.

'Yes, I'm sure. Don't interrupt, please. If I don't get it out in one go, I may not have the courage to finish. And hear all I have to say before you judge me.'

He took a deep breath, steeling himself, then he proceeded to relive the past.

'We weren't always rich you know. I was a very average accountant when we went to Summer Bay that year. I'd been promising your mother a holiday for so long but we never seemed to have the money. Going to the caravan park was a compromise; a break away without it being too expensive. So we headed off . . . the four of us.'

Amanda reacted. Four? She went to interrupt.

'No please,' Bernard hurried on, 'Remember what I asked. You had a sister you see, a twin sister. Julia. You'll understand it all in a minute.

'It was a wonderful few weeks. I never imagined life could be so good. Your mother was happier than I had ever known her to be. You and Julia were like two identical little dolls as you played on the beach. You were never apart, the two of you. You were like copies of the same person.'

Amanda suddenly realized who had been hidden inside the black hole of her dreams. Her sister. But how? How could she have forgotten this other half of herself? Why was the memory of her so threatening?

'Perhaps we were too happy. Who knows? Maybe some malicious demon looked down on us and decided that such happiness shouldn't be allowed to exist. Whatever the reason, we were struck by the most terrible tragedy. It was night. Your mother and I were just on the other side of the caravan park. We'd left you playing with two little locals, playing hide and seek. The three of you had found a space together in the dark under the caravan. Julia was looking for you. She went into the van. Perhaps she heard your giggles from underneath and thought you were inside. Who knows? What-ever the reason, she was in there alone. There was a cake on the table and she decided to sneak some.

'When your mother and I came into the van we found her on the floor. She was blue. It was a one in a billion chance. She'd choked on the cake and couldn't cough it up. Your mother became hysterical. Neither of us knew first aid, but I knew enough to know I had to clear her wind-pipe. I lost my head, I suppose. I went hysterical. I pounded on her chest. Pounded and pounded. Too hard. I was desperate you see. I didn't know my own strength. I crushed the poor little thing's ribs. Your mother was pulling at me, yelling: "Stop it Bernie! Stop it!"

'I only came to my senses when I heard you scream. You were standing in the doorway, screaming: "Don't kill her, Daddy, don't kill her!"

'I looked down and my little baby was limp, like a rag doll. She was dead.'

Bernard sighed, drained by the experience of recalling this horror.

'Our nightmare was only just beginning, though. People had heard your mother's cries; they'd heard you. They hurried in and found me crouched over Julia. Their evidence; the fact that I'd actually dislodged the cake from her windpipe so that the autopsy contradicted my story of her choking; the state of her poor little body; everything came together to make people suspect it was a case of child-bashing. There was such circumstantial evidence that it went to trial. I only got off because of the character witnesses, old friends who swore I was not the sort of man to hurt my child. There were plenty in Summer Bay who didn't know me and who believed I was guilty, who probably still do.'

'But why didn't you tell me? I'd have believed you . . . Sorry.'

She realized she had broken his request for silence.

'You were terribly scarred by the experience. You were so traumatized that you didn't speak for a year. What you'd seen . . . well . . . for a three-year-old who adored her sister . . . you were almost like one person . . . it was too much for you to cope with. We took you to the best child psychologists. There was nothing they could do. Then . . . one day you just spoke again. You can't imagine how happy your mother and I were. It was a single moment of joy in a horrific year. But even that joy was short-lived. We suddenly realized, from what you were saying, that you couldn't remember a thing about what happened. You'd blocked out the entire thing. You'd even blocked out the fact that there ever was a Julia. The doctors said we shouldn't force the memories, that they

should be left to come back of their own
accord.

'Everything that had been Julia's became
yours. It was as though she'd never existed;
as though there'd only ever been one little
girl in the house. And I suddenly realized
that I hoped you never would remember.
You'd seen me bending over her, you see.
You'd called out to me not to kill her.

'If she remembers, I thought, she'll think
what so many of the others thought. She'll
think that I killed her sister.

'Your mother and I had constant arguments
about it over the years. She wanted to tell
you so many times, but I was too scared.
The more time that passed, the more I convinced myself that you'd believe the worst,
that you'd turn against me as a murderer, if
you remembered.

'We moved, left all our old friends behind
us. New job, new home, new life. And, as if
to make up for what had happened, fortune
smiled on me. I had the Midas touch. All my
business schemes turned to gold. It only
took me four years to make my fortune. I
lived for work, and for you. Your mother
and I drifted apart. When she died . . . there
was nothing left of our marriage really. In a

way, our love died that day along with Julia.

'You became everything to me after that. You were all I had left. So you can imagine how terrified I was when you started asking questions. The doctors had warned me that the changes of puberty might remove the memory blocks. I didn't know what to think. All I could see was you turning against me. Even if you didn't think I killed Julia, I thought you might never forgive me for denying you the knowledge of her existence for so long. So . . . I did what I did. There are no excuses, except . . . my love for you I guess, and . . . my fear.'

He lapsed into silence. There was nothing more to say. He waited.

Had he lost his beloved daughter's love in these last few weeks of her life?

chapter eight

There were ten minutes to go before the afternoon bell. Matt tried to muster interest in the algebra problem in front of him.

He'd promised his mother that he'd work to make up the ground he had lost at school in the last months. He loved her too much to ignore the pain in her eyes as she sat him down for a talk.

'You can't go on like this, son,' she'd begun. 'Dad and me are real worried about you. We've got such hopes that you'll make something of yourself. It's too late for us to be anything except what we are.

'Not that we're unhappy,' she'd hastened to add. 'But you're a bright boy. You could go a long way if you tried. Don't let this one thing spoil your chances.'

'Maybe she's right,' thought Matt, as he tried to factorize a particularly difficult equation. 'I wish she could understand I can't help it, though.'

He sighed and looked at the clock at the front of the room. Only five minutes to go. He gave up.

'I'll do it at home tonight,' he thought.

He glanced out of the window and smiled to himself. There was Bobby Simpson, sneaking off early. He'd had a soft spot for Bobby, ever since that day long ago when she had rallied his fighting spirit. It saddened him to see her increasingly becoming the town rebel and outcast, the girl dubbed least likely to succeed. Still, she bore her misfortunes with a remarkably optimistic spirit.

'Maybe I should take a leaf out of her book,' he thought. The school P.A. system sputtered into life and Donald Fisher started the end-of-day announcements.

'It has been brought to my attention that a number of students have been absenting themselves from school before the final bell. Any student caught doing so, will find themselves on Saturday detention and yard duty for the next three weeks.'

'Bobby had better watch out,' Matt whispered to a boy across the aisle. 'She's going to cop it if she's not careful.'

But his attention was riveted back to the announcement, as Fisher continued.

'Would Matthew Wilson please come to my office immediately after the sounding of the bell? That is all. Ride your bikes carefully on the way home.'

There was a final crackle, as the sound system went dead.

'Who's gonna cop it?' His classmate grinned the question at him. 'What have you been up to, mate?'

Matt asked himself the same question, as he made his way to Fisher's office and knocked. Finding a Martian waiting for him would have been less of a surprise than the one he received.

'Mr Taylor wishes to speak to you privately, Matthew,' Fisher said grimly. 'I shall be outside if you need me, Mr Taylor.'

Matt felt his first twinge of unease as he registered Fisher's solemn expression. He was looking more than usually like an undertaker. He swung his gaze to Bernard Taylor as the door closed behind the stern deputy-head, and unease turned to apprehension. He could tell immediately from the man's expression that there was something very wrong. The bombastic, bulldog of a man who had had him arrested was gone. He was now pallid, drawn, diminished somehow.

'The first thing I have to do is apologize,' Bernard began softly. 'I treated you very shabbily the last time we met and I've thought very uncharitably of you since. I am not proud of the fact. I focussed all of my fears and insecurities on to you and chose to see you as a threat, not as just the young man in love that you were.'

'Are,' Matt corrected him softly. He didn't want the man thinking that his feelings had changed.

'Quite so.' Bernard nodded his head. 'I'm pleased to hear that. You'll understand why in a moment.'

He paused for a few seconds, to gather courage, then continued.

'I have no excuses for my behaviour. I can only hope that you will have the maturity to let bygones be bygones. I think you will agree, once I have told you why I'm here, that all that means very little now.'

In the next few moments, Matt's world slid away from beneath him. It couldn't be true?

It was, Bernard assured him, understanding the initial denial and anger that the boy was experiencing.

'It's exactly how I felt myself,' he told Matt,

wanting to place a comforting hand on his shoulder, but feeling restrained by the bitterness that had passed between them. 'But I quickly had to accept that feelings like that had to be pushed aside. Amanda has so little time left, that there is only time for love and understanding and . . . forgiveness. She has forgiven me, you see. I told her everything and she understood. I was such a fool not to have trusted her before. We're closer now than I ever thought possible. Just at a time when . . .'

He broke off. He didn't want to cry in front of the boy. He was here to imbue him with courage, not to wallow in self-pity.

'Amanda was admitted to the Summer Bay hospital. She wishes to die here, near to you, to her sister's grave, to where the whole family was so happy for one brief summer; before . . .'

He considered how to put it.

'. . . before the lies began, I suppose. She wants to see you.'

Matt was on his feet immediately. His mind was still spinning, but one thought rang out clearly above all the others. If Amanda needed him, he would be there. And he would give her all the strength and love he had.

The unlikely pair left the school a few moments later. Bernard's Rolls and driver were waiting outside, causing a stir amongst the kids.

'Hey, Wilson,' Alison Patterson called, as Matt and Bernard took their seats in the luxury car, 'D'ya win the lottery or something?'

'Talk about lucky,' she added to her friend Alyce.

The words rang ironically in Matt's ears as they drove in silence to the hospital. Lucky? The girl he loved had only a short time to live; he was being reunited with her so that he could watch her waste away and die. Was that lucky?

The car came to a halt and they walked quickly into the hospital. They stopped outside the door to Amanda's private room. Bernard hung back.

'You should go in alone. Be strong for her.'

He overcame his reserve and gripped Matt's hand.

'I'll see that you're not disturbed.'

Amanda had been lying in bed, waiting anxiously. Would Matt want to see her? Would he want to take on the burden of grief that getting involved again would entail?

'I can't blame him if he doesn't,' she thought, trying to buffer herself against disappointment. But, deep down, she knew that her heart would break if he didn't come.

The door opened and Matt appeared. He stood for a few moments, staring at her. She felt her heart start to pound, felt tears sting the corners of her eyes. But they were tears of joy, not of despair.

He moved across to her, wordlessly.

'Nothing needs to be said,' she thought. 'He knows that. He knows that words would only get in the way just now. They can come later.'

They joined hands, as a single tear slid down her cheek. He reached across, gently collected the drop of moisture and then raised his fingertip and kissed it. Then he lowered his lips to hers. He sat on the bed next to her, wrapped his arms around her and kissed her again, but this time deeply and passionately.

She closed her eyes and allowed herself to float in his embrace. Time stood still. There was no pain, there was no suffering, there was no death. For a brief moment, in his arms, she was immortal.

Matt hardly left Amanda's side for the next seven weeks. His parents gave him total freedom, he was given permission to absent himself from school whenever he chose to do so; he was in control of his own life until that inevitable day that they all dreaded.

He became very close to Bernard, the three of them spending hours together in Amanda's room, talking, playing games, laughing, crying when their grief overtook them, raging against fate when their mood swung in that direction.

All three were totally emotionally honest with each other. The time for lies and subterfuge was in the past, and this openness seemed to help Amanda face the great unknown of death that lay ahead of her.

She left the hospital twice in those weeks. Her first trip was with Bernard. He took her to her sister's grave. Nestled in a corner of the quaint and picturesque Summer Bay graveyard, was the tiny plot and the headstone.

IN LOVING MEMORY
OF
JULIA TAYLOR
1975–1978

Suffer the children to come unto me.

Bernard stood back at a distance and wept, as his daughter knelt at the grave of her long-dead twin.

Amanda bowed her head in prayer, asking Julia to be waiting to guide her on whatever journey lay ahead.

The second visit was with Matt. She went with him to the beach.

'I want to see you surf, just one more time,' she told him.

'I don't surf any more,' he said.

'Why not? You were so wonderful.'

'I don't know.' He shrugged. He didn't want to go into the complex psychology of it all.

'You musn't give it up. You've got to keep at it, for me, ' she begged him. 'That's how I always remembered you when I was in Switzerland; on a wave, laughing, happy. Please. Let me watch you surf again.'

The doctors had advised against it, Amanda was now so weak. But she'd insisted.

The sun was just peeping over the horizon, as they drove from the hospital to the beach. A number of the gang were already there, waxing up their boards, excited about the perfect sets that were rolling through. They looked up curiously at the incongruous sight of Bernard's Rolls with Matt's surfboard sticking out of the back window.

Jacko's eyes glowed with delight, as he saw his mate alight and walk down the beach towards them.

'Matt's here,' he said to the others, and began a slow and ritualistic handclap to welcome his friend back into their midst. The others joined in as Matt walked towards them.

He turned to where he could see the frail, pale form of his beloved Amanda watching from the car-park and raised his fist heavenward in triumph. He knew now that she had been right. He should never have turned his back on the sea.

Amanda watched him paddle out into the pounding waves. She smiled.

'I love him so, Daddy,' she told Bernard, who sat beside her holding her hand. 'I wish I could have grown up with him. I would have loved to have had his baby. I would have called it Julia if it had been a girl.'

Her vision started to fade, as she watched Matt take his first ride. As he sped across the perfectly formed wave, she suddenly felt light.

'Daddy, I love you.'

She felt herself lift from her body. She only had the strength left to say finally:

'Tell Matt I'll always be with him.'

'Amanda!'

Bernard's anguished cry came from a long distance. She was travelling down a long tunnel, at the end of which was a peaceful, inviting bright light. In the middle of the light was a beautiful, little three-year-old girl, who held her arms out invitingly. Amanda was filled with an incredible sense of peace.

'Julia,' she sighed.

And she felt herself being absorbed into the energy of all that was and all that will be. She and her beloved sister were together again.

It seemed like the entire town turned out for the funeral. Whether they knew Amanda or not, the story of the star-crossed lovers had captured the town's imagination. Word had naturally spread that Bernard Taylor was back in town, but Matt had made sure those who still thought the worst about Julia's death were put straight. The atmosphere at the graveside was one of total sympathy and support for both father and lover.

The funeral was at nine o'clock in the morning, an early hour to enable Matt to make the surfing competition that afternoon in Yabbie Creek. He and Amanda had talked about it the night before her death. She had urged him to enter, although she knew she would not be strong enough to attend. She wanted him to bring the trophy back to her, she had said, hoping in this way to spur him on to a win.

'Earth to earth, ashes to ashes, dust to dust.'

The words were meaningless to Matt. This was everyone else's farewell to Amanda. He had his own organized for later; a private one just between the two of them.

He looked around at the crowd. Celia, Betty and Doris dabbing their eyes with their handkerchiefs; Floss and Neville, Floss deriving no pleasure from having been so startlingly accurate in her prediction; Lance and Martin looking completely out of place in their Sunday best; Alf and Roo, Alf feeling the guilt of having wrongly accused Bernard for eleven years; Fisher, wearing his most solemn expression; Bobby, hovering at the edge of the crowd like the outcast that she was; Ailsa, exuding the solid decency that so totally characterised her; and finally his Mum and Dad, those two dear people who had always been there for him when he needed them.

He saw Bernard move forward, pick up a handful of dirt and throw it on to the coffin. He followed in his wake. Another empty gesture he thought. There was only one way for him to say goodbye to Amanda, the way that he knew she would want him to.

That afternoon, at the Yabbie Creek Surfing Competition, he rode like a man possessed. The crowd on the beach stood in awe, as the handsome blond boy blitzed the field in ride after skillful ride. And they wondered about his state of mind for, as he rode the final wave with private demons showing in every perfect move and turn, he cried to the wind with a voice full of anguish:

'Amanda!!!!'

Only his few friends knew the tragic truth.

The sun was setting when Matt moved into the graveyard. He carried the trophy in his hand. He knelt beside the grave and placed it gently in front of the headstone.

'This is for you,' he said. 'I love you.'

He whispered the last three words very gently. Then he lay down on the grave and wept as if his heart would break.

epilogue

Bobby sat at the top of a sand dune and stared miserably out to sea. She had felt down many times before in her life, but she'd never felt lower than she did right now.

She had been framed by Fisher for robbing his house, she'd been dobbed into the cops by the Fletchers, that pack of dorks who'd just bought the caravan park, and she was out on bail awaiting trial. If things went against her, and they always seemed to, she'd end up in a reform home.*

'How are you doing, Bob?'

Matt suddenly appeared behind her and sat down next to her. He was in his wetsuit and carried his board. He had just come from the surf, where Bobby had watched him for a while, before her troubles had absorbed all her attention.

* See 'The Bobby Simpson Story'

'I hear you've got a few problems,' he said.

Bobby smiled for the first time in days.

'Seems like we've been here before,' she replied. 'How old were we then?'

'Eleven. Guess the big difference is, you were the one doing the sympathizing back then.'

Matt, at seventeen, was the best looking guy in Summer Bay.

'Except maybe for that eldest kid at the caravan park,' thought Bobby. 'Frank or whatever his name is. Pity he's a Fletcher.'

She didn't want to think about that pack of creeps. She swung her thoughts back to Matt.

'Pity he's a blond. I could go for him if he had dark hair. It's funny how you only go for certain types. Not that I'd have a chance. No one has, the way he's never got over that Amanda chick. It's a bit creepy how he still goes out to her grave.'

'Don't you think?' Matt asked. He had been chatting on, unaware that she was deep in thought.

'Sorry?' She felt bad about being caught not listening.

'I was just saying how your being so positive all the time gave me someone to look up to.'

'You? Look up to me?' Bobby couldn't believe her ears. She was the town dero. Why would anyone look up to her?

'It was really hard for me after Amanda died. Sure, I had my folks, and her Dad kept in touch, but . . . I don't know . . . I thought I was going to go under a few times. And every time I nearly did, I thought about you. You've had so many kicks in the teeth and you've always come back fighting. You helped me, by . . . by being an example I suppose.'

Bobby felt really warm. No kid in town had ever said anything remotely as nice as this to her. And here was Matt, probably the guy in Summer Bay with the most going for him, telling her that she had helped him. Maybe she wasn't so useless after all.

'I called Mr Taylor,' Matt continued. 'I still get in touch with him every now and then. He's got friends in the legal profession and he's going to see that you get the best representation that there is.'

'Why . . .?' Bobby couldn't imagine what favours Bernard Taylor could possibly owe her.

'He's doing it for me,' Matt said. 'He's a pretty lonely man and I think he's glad that there's something he can do. I think he feels that Amanda would want him to do it. Anyway, that's all I wanted to let you know. Whatever lawyer he gets'll be in touch. Catch you later, eh?'

He got up to go.

'Hey!' Bobby wasn't very good at thank-yous. 'You're okay.'

'You're okay too, Bob.'

'Why?'

'Did I do it?'

'Yeah.'

Matt considered for a moment and then smiled.

'Because you were the first of the kids who saw me as anything other than the bin man's son. I guess I've owed you for six years.'

'Yeah, well I owe you now.'

'Let's call it evens.'

He walked away. Today was his day to visit Amanda and he didn't want to be late. He was always there by one o'clock. He'd tended her grave and polished up the trophy for three years now. It was almost a weekly ritual, but an emotionally important one.

He was out of metal polish, so he dropped into Ailsa's to buy some.

'A can of metal polish thanks, Ailse.'

'Coming up.' Ailsa was very fond of this fine young man. 'It astonishes me you know. Anyone'd think that trophy would have gone walkabout by now, sitting out there in that deserted graveyard.'

'I reckon everyone knows I'd come looking for anyone who took it. Besides,' his expression softened, 'Amanda's there. I know it sounds corny but, in a way I reckon she makes sure no one takes it.'

'Maybe you're right. There you go.'

She handed across the tin of polish and took his money. He restored her faith in young people; and more especially in love.

As Matt left the store, he found his way blocked by three girls; a cute little thing of about eight, a second dark-haired girl of about fourteen and a third attractive one who looked about his own age.

'Comin' through,' he said, as a warning to watch his surfboard. 'Gidday.'

There was something about the third girl that reminded him of Amanda; if only slightly. He glanced back at her. Yes, there was a definite resemblance.

165

As he walked into the graveyard, it struck him who the three girls must be. They'd be from the family who'd just moved into Alf's old place. Someone had said what the eldest girl's name was, mentioning that she would be in his class when the school year began.

Carly. That was it.

He sat down beside the grave, opened the can of metal polish and set to on the trophy. He liked to know that it was always there, shining and looking like it had the day he'd won it. Shining and fresh; just like his memories of Amanda.

But as he sat there, he felt his thoughts drifting to the girl he'd just seen. Carly. It was a nice name.

He suddenly felt guilty. This wasn't right. He always spent his time at the graveside thinking of the few happy days he and Amanda had shared together; the best days of his life.

A gentle breeze blew up and played amongst the trees. It made a rustling sound as it moved between the branches. And then he heard it. He would swear until his dying day that it had been a voice, although he never told anyone except Bernard Taylor. It was a whisper, part of the sound of the wind in the trees but separate from it. The voice was Amanda's. And the voice said one thing.

'Live. Live your life.'

He couldn't believe his ears. But then he heard it again, just as the wind faded, clear as a bell from out of the moan made by the breeze.

Yes, it was her! It was Amanda!!!

His eyes filled, as he placed the trophy back on the grave, stood and walked out of the cemetery for the last time.

For he knew that she had given her blessing to whatever the rest of his life held for him.

He knew at last that he could move on.

THE HOME AND AWAY SERIES

The **Home And Away** TV show is one of the most successful soaps ever to hit the screens and, as prequels to the gripping television saga, the following books tell the stories of your favourite characters prior to the TV series.

The Carly Morris / Steven Matheson Stories   **0140 901531**

From the day she was born Carly Morris' existence has been blighted by the atrocious acts of a sadistic father and a malicious twin sister. Now in her mid-teens, life for Carly becomes a battle to keep her sanity and to stay alive. Steven Matheson has a different but no less difficult struggle. He has to fight against malignant outside influences, thieves and school thugs, which threaten to destroy the happiness of his family life.

The Bobby Simpson Story
0140 901272

Bobby Simpson, having been deserted by her real mother, is brought up by parents she believes are her own. Forced to suffer rough treatment at the hands of her adoptive father and being victimised by the deputy head of her school makes Bobby rebel in the only way she can. Bobby is to grow from being a wild tomboy to a deeply troubled young woman yearning for security and love.

The Frank Morgan Story
0140 901280

Frank Morgan's father is a criminal, his mother an alcoholic and Frank is running wild. At the age of 8 he tries to prove himself to his father by robbing a bank. But the police catch up with the boy and he is taken away from home and sent into care. The Fletcher family try hard to make Frank's life a happier one but unfortunately his troubles are not destined to end so soon.

Mr Majeika's Magical TV Fun Book   0140 901981

Mr Majeika is back again with stories, jokes, recipes and games to play with your friends. Follow the antics of your favourite wizard from Walpurgis as he helps to save a family of foxes, narrowly escapes having to marry an ugly mermaid and clambers over icy rooftops to lend Santa a hand in three spellbinding adventures.

Skateboarding Is Not A Book　　　　　　　　**0140 900349**

Whether you are a novice "street" skater or a highly paid
professional skateboarding star this book is for you.
Skateboarding is an obsession and a way of life for millions of
people all over the world – and it's GROWING. Skateboarding
Is Not A Book covers everything you need to know about the
sport – its history, the equipment you need and where to find it,
where to skate, injuries and those crucial skills and techniques.